RISKIER

A CROSSING THE LINE NOVELLA

BUSINESS

TESSA BAILEY

Entangled Publishing, LLC
2614 South Timberline Road
Suite 109
Fort Collins, CO 80525
Visit our website at www.entangledpublishing.com.

Select Suspense is an imprint of Entangled Publishing, LLC.

Edited by Heather Howland
Cover design by Heather Howland and Amber Shah
Cover art from Shutterstock

Manufactured in the United States of America

First Edition January 2015

Chapter One

Ruby Elliott bent low over the pool table, lining up her shot on the six ball. She could feel the familiar, level gaze burning over her back, bottom, and thighs. Familiar, yes. But since the night all those months ago when she'd met her boyfriend, Troy Bennett, the power of that gaze had only strengthened, making it damn hard to concentrate on what she was doing. What game was he playing? He'd walked into Hildebrand's, her old Brooklyn neighborhood's local pool hall, twenty minutes ago, but instead of greeting her with a kiss as usual, he'd sat at the bar and ordered a beer. He'd been watching her ever since, steadily sipping from the bottle as though formulating a plan. Anticipation quivered in her belly, hot and liquid. Whatever he had planned, she needed him to hurry.

From day one, their relationship had never been anything less than exciting. Explosive. Often volatile. Could one expect anything less between a stubborn pool hustler and an NYPD detective who thrived on exercising control?

Their first week together had found them on opposite sides of the law. Troy had been investigating a local Brooklyn mobster, a man who just happened to be the father of her childhood best friend. Knowing the level of violence this man was capable of, she'd defected to Troy's side in an effort to keep him alive—and it had very nearly ended with a bullet in her reckless backside. Troy had saved her, though. In more ways than one. Not only had she stopped putting herself in danger to make money by fleecing marks out of their cash on the felt, she'd opened her own custom pool cue factory, and the business had taken off.

Finally, *finally*, she was exactly where she wanted to be.

After banking the eight ball, Ruby set her stick aside to rerack. Just as she finished the familiar task, she felt Troy move up behind her, brushing against her slightly as he passed. Electricity raced across her skin, every nerve ending in her body waking up and paying attention.

"Looking for a game?" he murmured near her ear.

Ruby shrugged, trying to appear unaffected, yet knowing her red cheeks likely gave her away. Her body never failed to betray her to this man. "Can you afford to play with me?"

He rested his hands on either side of her on the table, bringing his chest flush against her back. Deep in his throat he made a humming sound when his lap fitted snugly against her bottom. Ruby barely held back the urge to shift her body, tempt him closer. "I don't think I can afford not to," he said. "What's your name, little hustler?"

So this was his game. Pretend they didn't know each other? She could play along. Troy never did anything without a purpose. And his purpose was *always* her pleasure. "Ruby." She tilted her neck to the side, felt his gaze move lower to where her breasts strained against her tank top. "Why don't you put your money where your mouth is, then?"

His chest rumbled with a growl, alerting her to the fact that she was now playing with fire. Troy's dangerous fire. Her thighs squeezed together of their own accord. "I would worry about your own mouth if I was you. Before it gets you into trouble."

"Maybe I like trouble," she whispered.

"Well, you've definitely found it." One hand traveled to her hip, fingers digging in, just hard enough to make her gasp. "My brand of trouble is so good it hurts. You want to hurt a little tonight, baby?"

A blast of desire ricocheted through her system. She felt stripped bare, unsuited for a public place. The raucous conversations taking place in the bar had faded into background noise, Hildebrand's ceasing to exist around her. Troy frequently had this effect on her mind and body, leaving her struggling to contain her composure. "The only thing that's going to hurt is your ego when I beat you."

His laughter against her neck was filled with dark promises. "I think we know who's going to win in the end."

She swallowed hard. "You're very confident."

"Yeah. I am. Do you know why?" Troy pressed his hips close. She could feel his substantial erection, thick against her behind. "I have what makes you moan. What's going to make those thighs open wide. I've got it right here and you're fucking dying for it." He backed away and a whimper escaped Ruby before she could stop it. "Your break, hustler."

"What do I get if I win?" Ruby asked with forced nonchalance, even as her pulse kicked into high gear. Watching Troy play pool always turned her on to a stunning degree. He'd never let on until recently exactly what an accomplished player he was. *That* is what made her so hot. He didn't need to brag, nor did he pout like most men inevitably did when she won, which happened to be the majority of the time.

No. Troy took his victories elsewhere.

Ruby broke the rack, but divested of her concentration, sunk none of the balls. She narrowed her eyes at Troy's smirk as he approached the table.

He stopped in front of her, chalking his cue slowly. When he set the blue cube aside, his stormy blue gaze found hers, voice dropping to a whisper. "If you win, I'll stop tonight when you beg me to."

Ruby inhaled shakily, resisting the urge to press a hand to her tightened belly. "And if you win?"

Troy laughed under his breath. "I don't stop. We go another round. Harder. So much fucking harder than the first one." He leaned in and ran his lips up the side of her neck, scraped his teeth against her heated flesh on the way back down. "How does that sound?"

Ruby was forced to lean her weight onto the pool cue in her hand when her legs would no longer support her. "I need to know exactly what *harder* entails before I agree to the bet." The temptation to hear more proved too much. Ruby suspected the more she pushed, the longer he would make her wait for satisfaction, but then curiosity had always been her downfall. "I deal in specifics."

"I don't appreciate being questioned," Troy murmured against her ear. "But I'll make an exception since we're getting to know each other." He moved to block her view of the bar. Gripping the front waistband of her jeans, he twisted it hard in his fist. Denim, already snug against her center, squeezed tight around that incredibly sensitive part of her until she gasped. Suddenly, release loomed so close, she knew if she moved her hips in either direction, she'd come right where she stood, in a bar full of people. A sensual, knowing smile played on his lips. "You want specifics? Fine. I'm going to fuck you in the shower. The neighbors can't hear you scream quite as loudly in there. I'm going to nail you, over and over, against the wall. Until you can't think. Or stand. Or speak." He twisted the denim even tighter and Ruby moaned into his shoulder. "Then I'm going to go down on you, lick the spot I just satisfied, pick you up, and do it all over again."

Troy released her waistband and Ruby slumped against the stool beside her. He maintained eye contact with her as he bent over the table and sunk a solid in the side pocket. As she watched, pulse jackhammering in her ears, Troy cleared the table of every ball except for hers, before knocking in the eight.

"Get your jacket."

· · ·

Ruby tossed her jacket onto the kitchen table, watching warily as Troy did the same. On the ride from Brooklyn back to Manhattan, he hadn't spoken to her once, communicating instead through discreet touches and hidden glances in the backseat of the cab. A hand brushing across her breasts, a soft growl beside her ear. The air between them practically vibrated, the electric hum matched by her own anxiousness. Still, the part of her brain that managed to think clearly around a sexually charged Troy had decided he wouldn't win the game quite so easily.

"Nice place you've got here," Ruby remarked casually, catching the slight twitch of his lips. She ran her fingers over the square red candles arranged in the center of the table. "I would say it needs a woman's touch, but it looks like somebody beat me to it."

Flash of amusement long gone, Troy rounded the table purposefully, crowding her against it. "Speaking of a woman's touch…" He took her hand and pressed it against his straining fly. "I'm done waiting for yours."

As he leaned in to kiss her, Ruby drew back quickly. His low sound of frustration made her stomach muscles clench. Teasing a hungry Troy was like juggling a stick of lit dynamite. Too bad she was about to clue him in to the fact that his plan to pretend they didn't know each other had backfired. "Just a minute, big boy. I don't sleep with men I just met." She leaned back on the table, letting her shirt ride up to expose her belly. "I'm going to need a little convincing."

A muscle worked in his jaw. "Convincing."

Ruby bit her lip and nodded. "I need to know what kind of man I've allowed to bring me home."

Troy's gaze dropped to her bare midriff. "You should be careful what you wish for." He braced himself with hands on either side of her hips, then bent low to let his warm breath fan across her belly. Such a simple action, yet Ruby's lips parted on a shaky sigh, thighs tightening on top of the table. Before she could guess his intention, he bared his teeth and ripped open the button on her jeans. He hit her with blistering eye contact, maintaining it as he drew down her zipper, painstakingly slow, with his teeth. Her shuddering breaths echoed in the kitchen as Troy straightened to his full height once more. "You want to know what type of man I am, Ruby?"

"Yes," she whispered.

So fast she didn't have time to react, his big hand disappeared inside the opening of her jeans, shoving her panties aside to impale her with his middle finger. When Ruby automatically moaned and tipped her head back, legs opening in a silent plea, Troy sucked in a breath. "I'm the kind of man who makes you *this* goddamn wet before he's even touched you." He withdrew his hand and turned toward the bathroom, pulling his shirt over his head as he went. Seeing his broad, sinfully defined back revealed, Ruby's pulse sped up even faster. "When you're ready to stop playing games, come get in the shower."

Ruby stripped off the last of her clothes, leaving them in a pile outside the bathroom door. She could hear Troy on the other side, pulling back the shower door and stepping under the pounding spray, interrupting its flow. Eager to see hot water spill down his back, soak his body, she nudged the door open with her toe. Her breathing went shallow with anticipation, heat mingling with impatience in her belly. She'd waited long enough. Couldn't wait any longer to be taken by him.

She took a single step into the bathroom and stopped, concern overriding every other emotion. Troy stood naked beneath the coursing water, hands braced high against the tile wall. His shoulders and back, so flawlessly sculpted it ached to look at them, were unusually stiff. Rigid with tension. He'd bowed his head forward slightly, but Ruby could see his eyes were closed. His jaw tight.

"Troy?"

Immediately, he straightened. As if he hadn't expected her to enter the bathroom behind him so quickly. As if she could wait. When he turned to her, Ruby's chest went tight. Anxiety. Dread. Love. All three emotions waged a battle on his face. Then just as quickly, his expression went blank. He held out his hand to her, gaze tracking down her naked body slowly. Heating. Planning.

"Come here."

She slid her palm over Troy's, let him help her over the rim of the tub. Ease her against his hard body.

Using his hips, he pushed her back onto the slick wall, lips moving over her neck. "Help me take away the ache, baby. You know how bad it gets when I don't fuck you in the morning."

Ruby wanted so badly to forget the look she'd seen on his face. The trepidation she'd witnessed. But her love for this man wouldn't allow her to leave him hurting for some unnamed reason. To distract her with her one weakness. Himself. When he leaned in to kiss her, she placed a hand on his chest to hold him back. "Something's wrong." Her whisper was nearly swallowed by the pelting water. "Talk to me, first."

His eyes squeezed shut, then opened slowly, containing

a predatory glint. She couldn't shake the intuition he was hiding something, but when he hit her with the full force of his magnetism, her thoughts tended to scatter. And he well knew it. "Talk to you?" His hands molded to her bottom and lifted, seating her on top of his slippery erection, levering her against the wall with the use of his hips. Ruby moaned, ankles automatically locking behind his back. "What would you like to hear? That my girlfriend has become my obsession? That I can't think past getting inside her? Every. Single. Hour." He punctuated each word with a devastating upward thrust, then kissed her hard, tongue moving over hers, claiming her. She felt his mood shift rapidly as his mouth ravished hers. From seductive to desperate. It sent warning signals to her brain. "I won't let you go. I won't let you go back to that," he rasped. The kiss deepened briefly, *fiercely*. "Have to keep you *safe*."

Somehow his words broke through the fogbank of lust, dragging Ruby back to where she could breathe. "Let me go, Troy? Go back to where?"

He buried his face against her neck, his chest rising and falling with rapid breaths. She wrapped her arms around him and held him close, trying to stifle her alarm and failing.

His tortured gaze finally met hers. "Your father is back in town."

Chapter Two

Troy felt Ruby go completely still against him. Where seconds earlier she'd been wet and pliant, her body had grown stiff, her expression guarded. Reminiscent of how she'd looked the first time they'd met, when she'd been hustling for a living. When she'd been distrusting of everyone and everything. Especially a cop like him. That distrust had almost ripped her away from him. After his job and her criminal past bleeding together had caused her to literally *bleed*, he'd vowed never to let anything harmful touch her again. Here it was, though. Too soon. Right on their doorstep.

In a move that only increased his disquiet, her legs went limp, dropping from around his waist, her hips twisting to unlock their bodies. It alarmed him, this automatic shield she raised. As if he needed another reason to be fucking anxious or worried for her safety. The safety he'd worked so damn hard to achieve. After leaving the pain of losing his best friend and partner behind back in Chicago, his fear of loss had been challenged by a pool hustler who never looked before she leaped. Ruby had finally met him halfway after months of compromise, and with the utterance of a single sentence, he felt it slipping away. If he didn't think it would scare her, he'd have already put his fist through the bathroom wall.

Helplessness was a living thing inside him. Briefly this afternoon, he'd considered not telling Ruby about Jim Elliott's return. One look at his rap sheet told Troy he could easily have her father picked up for some bullshit misdemeanor. He had outstanding warrants in several states, and had violated his probation by leaving New York in the first place. Troy could have used the threat of imprisonment to send Jim packing. Out of Brooklyn. Away from his daughter, who'd finally managed to get her life together despite her father's atrocious parenting skills.

Ruby would have never been the wiser.

He'd picked up the phone several times to make the call, but ultimately couldn't do it. If she ever found out, they might not recover from the betrayal. Trust was everything between them, and Troy wouldn't violate it, no matter how much he hated seeing the strongest person he knew shrink before him when presented with her greatest weakness.

Her love for a man who'd neglected her, endangered her, then abandoned her.

"What...what did he want?" Ruby asked numbly.

Troy hesitated for a split second and she tensed, trying to move farther away. Visibly angry at him for even considering holding back. He gripped her arms and kept her still. "He wants to see you." The words felt like they were strangling him. "He...it sounds like he has some sort of proposition."

Tell her I've got an offer she'll want to hear, specifically.

"Oh."

Looking down at her shell-shocked expression, he wanted to rage at the unfairness of it. Since graduating from business school, Ruby had found an investor to get her custom pool cue business off the ground. It had taken off virtually overnight, her skill perfected by her own experience playing the game and connections she'd made with pool players over the years. After one of her designs was featured in a billiards magazine last month, an article he'd framed and hung in their bedroom, she'd been buried with requests for her unique custom designs. Troy was so damn proud of her, of everything she'd done despite the disadvantages of her upbringing. She'd finally come into her own. Now this news had swung in like a wrecking ball, threatening to dismantle it all.

Troy knew from experience he had to handle the situation very carefully. Knowing Ruby, her mind was already racing behind her stunned features. Weighing options. Making plans. Her first instinct would be to keep him out of whatever her father wanted her to do. *Over my cold, lifeless body.* His first obstacle would be her stubborn desire to keep him separated from her past. She *was* her past. It had shaped her, molded her, made her streetwise at too young of an age. Since he wanted every single part of her, keeping him out of it wouldn't be happening.

His second obstacle would be making sure she didn't get sucked back into her old life. While he knew Ruby was too smart to resume the illegal activities she'd worked so hard to leave behind, family could be a powerful thing. Ruby had always been too loyal for her own good.

Apprehension churned in his gut. Something in Jim Elliott's confident swagger, his casual smirk, told Troy he had an ace up his sleeve. For now, he needed to push his dark fears aside and focus on Ruby. One hurdle at a time. It was how they approached every problem that came along with a cop and a hustler being in a committed relationship. Careful compromise.

He cupped her face, tipping it upward. Unfocused eyes looked right through him, until he brought their foreheads together. "Hey. Everything is going to be okay. We're going to talk about this, but I need you to look at me. Actually *look* at me." She blinked once, nodded. Slowly, awareness crept back over her features and Troy's panic eased slightly. "I'm not going to try to talk you out of meeting with him."

A dark eyebrow arched. He had her attention now. "Really."

"Yes. We both know you've already decided, anyway." Her gaze darted away and Troy bit back a sigh. "My only condition is you don't shut me out. I go with you. You and I deal with whatever he says together."

A battle waged inside Ruby. He could see it in every tense line of her body. She squeezed her eyes shut, shaking her head. "No," she choked out. "No, Troy. You have to let me handle this. He's my father. Nothing he says will convince me to go back. You'll have to trust me on that."

He'd been expecting this, Troy reminded himself. No need to feel this pain over her trying to close him out. Her need to protect him, protect those she cared about, was simultaneously her greatest strength and weakness. He'd anticipated it. He'd lived through it once before. And his memory of almost losing her the first time remained too fresh. So he'd come prepared to play hardball. "You keep me involved, Ruby, or I get him put away." He ignored the shocked betrayal radiating from her. "I trust you to make the right call, but I don't trust *him*. I will find a way to keep you safe. How I accomplish that is up to you."

She wanted to be mad at him, he could tell. But it wouldn't stick. Not when he'd let his walls drop, let her glimpse the fear on his face. He hid nothing. It was the only way to get through to her. Let her see his determination to protect her. How much he loved her. Her rigid posture softened gradually as they stared hard at each other. A breath shuddered past her lips. "Dammit. This feels too familiar. We're not back in that place already, are we?"

His grip on her arms tightened. "No. We are not back there. We're *here*. We're stronger." He slid a hand through her hair, spoke against her temple. "We'll be weaker apart. Don't let him separate us."

"Troy—"

He cut her off with his mouth. Perhaps it was wrong, but he was so close to gaining her acceptance that he used the last, and most powerful, weapon in his arsenal. It couldn't be helped. He was desperate. For her promise *and* her body. Deepening the kiss until she moaned low in her throat, Troy braced his hands on either side of her head. He dipped his knees and dragged his wet body up against Ruby's, tempting her back with the feel of his ready cock between her legs, sliding up her belly. He meshed them together, chest to thigh. *We're one, baby. We're stronger together.* When Troy curled his hands beneath her knees with the intention of levering her against the tile wall once more, she broke away.

Breathing heavily, lips swollen, she looked too goddamn beautiful for words. *My woman.* "Wait. I-I just want to say…I know it wasn't easy for you, telling me this. To not try to talk me out of the meeting. Thank you." Her mouth moved over his, robbing his clarity. "You're right. This is nothing like last time. We're better." Hearing those words coming from Ruby felt like a balm to his soul. It comforted the insecurities he still harbored over keeping her. It must have shown, because her eyes softened. He leaned into her hand as she stroked the side of his face. "Were you feeling out of control today, Troy?"

Jaw clenched, he nodded, but didn't answer. Couldn't answer. She'd nailed his issue squarely on the head. It was no secret between them that he craved control. Usually, he took it in the bedroom, but it often reached into other aspects of their life together. Something he'd been working on. It hadn't been easy for him today, relinquishing the need to handle her problem without troubling her for one second with it. He'd managed to be completely open with her, knowing it was right. But he wouldn't pretend that having her recognize and appreciate his difficult position didn't fill him with male pride.

Nimble fingers played on his chest, stroked down over his abdomen. His breathing harshened, echoing through the shower. Her mouth followed the path her fingers made, licking at water droplets, until she dropped to her knees in front of him. From her kneeling position, she looked up at him with complete trust, mingled with need. "Take back your control, Troy."

He groaned loudly, finally giving in to the urge to connect his fist to the wall. She knew what he needed, was giving him back his power. *Fuck*, he loved her. Tonight at Hildebrand's, he'd struggled to balance himself. Meeting Ruby's father, knowing instinctively his return could bruise their relationship, he'd played a game with Ruby. It had put him in the driver's seat for a while longer. He should have known it wasn't necessary. That she would see right through him.

She dragged her nails up his thighs, kissed his shuddering stomach, waiting for him to direct her. Her beauty never failed to mesmerize him, but her inner strength battered his heart. As always, her relinquishing that power shot straight to his head. Lust, already heady and thick, burned brighter until nothing existed but the two of them, surrounded by steam in their shower. The change spread through him. The transformation she'd taught him to welcome instead of dread. With a steady hand, he wrapped her thick black hair in his fist and tilted her face up.

"Mouth open. Eyes on me."

Those beautiful red lips parted without hesitation. Only once did her gaze leave his, dropping to his heavy erection. Looking at it with a blatant hunger that sizzled through his nerve endings. When she groaned a little and shifted her hips as if impatient, his grip tightened in her hair until she gasped. Using his other hand, he guided himself to her mouth, but stopped an inch away.

"Tell me how bad you want it."

Her eyelids fluttered. "Very badly."

Dragging the head of his cock across her parted lips, the movement deliberately slow, he spoke in a deeper, more commanding voice than just moments before. "I told you to think about sucking me today while you worked. Did you do as I asked?"

She nodded, whimpering in pleasure when he slipped himself partially into her mouth, let her lips suction around him, then withdrew despite her sound of protest. Most men would find this anticipation torture, but he craved it like a drug. The longer he waited for release, the harder it rocked him. If it didn't torture his woman in the process, he would stand there and tease her mouth for hours, denying himself. Denying her. It was another reason he'd initiated the game tonight, to delay gratification, build the need. Now, however, he couldn't hold out. He'd been lost at sea today and pleasure wouldn't wait much longer.

"When you thought about having me in your mouth, did you want to touch yourself?"

A hitch in her breath caused his eyes to narrow. Needing to hear her answer, he withdrew from her lips, pulse pounding loudly in his ears. So painfully aroused that his legs felt strong and unsteady at the same time. "Did you touch yourself, Ruby?"

"Yes. I was alone at the workshop...when I thought of you, I couldn't stop. I had to."

His erection grew more stiff and demanding with every whispered word, the need for release nearly bringing him to his knees. Images of Ruby touching herself swam in his head, each more erotic than the last. He knew from experience that when she brought herself to orgasm with her own hand, her eyes went blind and her entire body shook. Not nearly as fiercely as when she climaxed around his cock, but incredibly hot to witness and impossible to forget.

Dying for just one second of relief, reeling from her confession, Troy pushed himself past her swollen lips and sank deep, right to the point he knew she could take him. "How does that taste, baby?"

She hummed in her throat, her mouth working him in long strokes. When she took him deep, deeper into her throat than she ever had before, he groaned at the ceiling and pulled out. Any longer and he'd come. A pleasure he wouldn't allow himself until he'd seen to her needs. Still, he allowed her to lick at the tip while he satisfied his curiosity.

"When you came today, what were you thinking about? Was I filling your mouth?"

She paused in her ministrations, appearing to choose her words. "Yes. In the beginning."

His fascination grew. "What happened in the end?"

Her eyes locked with his, darkened. "It always ends with you inside me."

"That's fucking right," he grated. "And in between?"

After a slight hesitation, she reached past him and returned holding the long-handled wooden back scrubber. Teeth sinking into her bottom lip, she ran a single finger down the smooth side of the object, then looked up at him, vulnerability and anticipation warring on her face. Troy's stomach muscles tightened so swiftly, he groaned, nearly climaxing right then, she'd shocked and pleased him so thoroughly. He took the wooden scrubber from her hand. Based on her accelerated breathing, he knew his expression told her everything she needed to know. That she'd just sent him past the point of obsession.

"Turn around. Get on your knees and brace yourself against the wall with your hands."

Visibly shaking, she did as he instructed. Troy took a long moment to savor the picture she made, her smooth back and gorgeous ass presented to him like a goddamn gift. He fisted his erection and squeezed, knowing when he finally got inside her, after giving her what she'd so boldly requested, he'd be frantic. As if he'd ever been anything but frantic to fuck Ruby. Every chance he got.

He traced the line of her back, the curve of her bottom with the smooth wood, letting it dip between her thighs for a moment. She moaned throatily, but he interrupted the beautiful sound with the wet slap of damp wood on equally wet flesh. He waited a beat for her reaction, to gauge the amount of strength he could put behind the strikes without taking away the pleasure and leaving only pain. She cried out and arched her back, her body begging for more. Troy gripped the wood tighter and brought it down again, harder, groaning at the pink outline it left behind. That *he'd* left behind.

"Daydreaming about punishment, hustler?" *Slap.* "Have I not spanked you enough lately?"

"You have…I-I just—"

"Do I need to start making regular trips to your workshop to spank and fuck you? If you want it raw three times a day, Ruby, just say the word. I'll give it to you as often as you need it."

"Yes. More. Even *more*."

"Consider it done," Troy growled.

He watched her fingers straighten and flex against the wall with each blow, her moans increasing in volume until he wasn't so certain anymore about the neighbors not being able to hear them. Troy realized then that his own shouts of pleasure had joined hers. He could hardly stand due to the overwhelming necessity to be inside his woman.

Troy tossed the brush onto the bathroom floor and fell to his knees behind Ruby. She looked over her shoulder at him and his head rushed when he saw the blistering arousal on her face. Eyes half open, lips bruised from biting into them with her teeth, damp hair stuck to her neck and forehead. If he hadn't already been on his knees, she would have put him there with that single look.

In one swift move, he seated himself inside her, savoring her scream. Gritting his teeth, he gave her a moment to adjust to him, something she still required whenever they made love in this position. The one that got him so damn deep. He loved it. Those few moments of forcing himself to wait for that first perfect thrust. Months ago, when they'd both gotten tested and Ruby had gone on the pill, that careful control had eluded him for weeks, but he'd finally regained it. Even if the experience of loving her without an albeit-thin barrier still rocked him to the core every *single* time.

One of her hands left the wall to dig her fingernails into the skin of his thigh, a silent plea for him to move. He knew neither of them would last long after the evening's buildup, what they'd done, what she'd revealed. So he threw his head back and worked his hips in slow yet demanding circles, felt her start to close up on his cock.

"Good girl. Come for your man. Don't make me wait."

The backs of her thighs began to shake; her shoulders followed. Fuck, he was strung so tight after the events of the day, he couldn't hold back. He brought his palm down on her ass with a loud *smack* and sent her over the edge. Troy followed almost immediately, driving into her a final time before drowning in the bliss of her. Feeling drained and fulfilled at the same time, Troy pulled her upright, back against his chest, and held her tight.

He kissed her neck, closing his eyes when she pressed closer. Drenched and kneeling in the shower, it felt as though they were two survivors of a storm. But deep down, he knew the storm was only beginning.

"I love you, Ruby. We're going to be all right."

He wouldn't let it be any other way.

Chapter Three

Ruby pushed her goggles onto her forehead and turned off the wood lathe when Mya Hicks signaled her from across the workshop. She raised a questioning eyebrow at the woman who, in a short space of time, had gone from unexpected investor to friend, business partner, and coworker.

"I'm ordering lunch. You want?"

She pretended to consider a moment. "Chicken salad on wheat. Extra pickles. Diet Coke."

"You read my mind."

Ruby shook her head. They ordered the same thing for lunch every day. Asking had turned into a mere formality. She slipped her goggles back on and resumed her work on a cue that was due in Dallas by week's end. The customer had requested a naked woman etched into the handle. Had even sent her a picture of his girlfriend to work with. Pool players were superstitious and often eccentric, so she'd grown used to the odd requests. It wasn't her place to question. With the amount of money she charged, they could ask her to carve a naked Santa Claus and she wouldn't bat an eyelash. In fact, she'd done it just yesterday.

She glanced up from her work long enough to watch Mya hang up the phone and resume work at her desk, cataloging custom orders, filling out invoices, and ordering the supplies Ruby needed to create her designs. Not for the first time, she acknowledged how out of place Mya looked behind a desk completing paperwork. With a shock of pink running through her haphazard dark hair, and a tattoo sleeve twining up her right arm, she looked more like an artist. Or a biker. Basically, the furthest from a paper pusher that one could get. In her midforties, Mya had struck Ruby as a free spirit upon first glance. Although she looked young for her age and acted even younger, there was a knowledge in her eyes to which Ruby could relate. While Mya was certainly a beautiful woman, her looks didn't seem to sit comfortably with her. As if she would shed them in a heartbeat if it were possible.

When her college professor came to her and claimed he knew an investor willing to take a chance on her fledgling business idea, she'd been naturally wary. The ink on her business school diploma hadn't even dried. It had seemed too good to be true. When they'd been introduced, her curiosity had only grown. The word "investor" connoted a man with a briefcase. Not a rock star look-alike with a Korn beanie and ripped jeans. Yet they'd connected immediately. As they'd met and outlined their business model and strategy, Ruby had eventually stopped waiting for the other shoe to drop. Mya was noticeably standoffish about her past, but then, so was Ruby. No one wanted to invest their money in an ex–pool hustler, right? And obviously, Mya had her own demons on her tail. So through an unspoken agreement, they left the past off the table.

Which meant there was no way in hell she'd tell Mya her father had returned. Or what that could mean. Thankfully, she'd had the foresight to put Mya's name on the workshop lease, so no matter what resources he had at his disposal, he wouldn't be able to track her down there.

Pushing the relentless worry aside, Ruby finished her task and set the nearly finished cue on a rack just in time for their lunch to be delivered. She tossed her goggles on a workbench and went to join Mya at her desk. "Any new orders come in this afternoon?"

Mya took a long swig of her Diet Coke. "Four."

"Shit. I'm going to have to start working weekends."

"Or hire more people."

Ruby glanced at the medium-size workshop she'd so carefully arranged and decorated. Her pride and joy. Space she'd only ever dreamed of being able to afford. "I don't know if I'm ready to share yet. I'll think about it."

"You do that." Mya propped her booted foot on her knee, sandwich in hand. "Although I'm not sure Troy would appreciate you missing in action more than you already are."

"Oh? What makes you say that?" Ruby questioned sarcastically. Mya had met Troy on several occasions. Most of them included him watching Ruby work for an hour, growing impatient when she refused to take a break, then carrying her out of the workshop over his shoulder.

"Just a hunch."

"Right."

Mya laughed and patted her jeans pocket, searching for cigarettes that were no longer there since she'd quit recently. "Next time I see him, I'm going to ask him to set me up with a nice, chubby cop. Someone a little grateful, you know? Heck, I'll take a meter maid. I'm not a proud woman."

Ruby snorted. "Liar."

"That's fair." She bit into her sandwich with gusto. "But I can put my pride aside for the night. Tell Troy, the rounder the better. Just a big old chunk of man, named Ruben. Or Hank."

"Hold on. Let me write this down," Ruby joked. "You

might be able to tell him yourself. He, uh...mentioned he was going to try to stop by the shop more often."

"Why does that make you blush?"

"Not blushing." Ruby grabbed her drink and pushed off the desk. "Get your eyes checked."

"You seem better."

Goggles in hand, she turned back with a confused expression. "Better?"

Mya cleared her throat, looking a little uncomfortable. She leaned forward over her desk, suddenly engrossed in something on the computer screen. "This morning, when you came in. You were all quiet. I had Slipknot playing for an hour and you didn't scream at me to turn it off."

Ruby shook her head and fired up the lathe, ignoring the sense that Mya was still watching her curiously. She threw a smile over her shoulder. "Maybe I was just humoring you for once. I've never been better."

Apparently she hadn't managed to keep her apprehension from showing. After her night with Troy, where he'd reassured her over and over that everything would be all right, she felt marginally better. Nothing, however, could alleviate the dread in her gut. She'd agreed to let Troy contact her father to arrange a meeting for tomorrow night. Until the meeting was over, she knew nothing would shake the dark cloud of fear following her around. Despite her reassurances to Troy, she knew her father better than anyone in the world. They'd spent years together on the road, bilking people out of their money on the pool table. It had been necessary to know every aspect of each other's personality. To read each other. In order to be successful, they'd been required to know each other's move before it was even made. If he wanted Ruby to do something for him, he wouldn't have come unprepared. Deep down inside, she knew he'd somehow found a weakness. A way to draw her back in. It's how he operated.

In Ruby's back pocket, her cell phone vibrated. She dug it out and looked at the screen.

Spoke to Jim. Tomorrow night at eight. Quincy's. I'll be right there with you. Love, Troy.

With a shaking hand, she replaced her phone. He'd be right there with her to turn down her father's request. She believed him in that regard.

What would he do if she agreed?

. . .

Troy held the door of Quincy's open so Ruby could precede him. Tension radiated from the hard lines of his body as he scanned the bar. They were ten minutes late to meet her father, a power move she'd made on purpose. By not arriving on time, she hoped to communicate that she wouldn't jump when he asked. Second, being late to a meeting of this nature always put the waiting party on edge. As Ruby searched Quincy's for her father's lanky frame and thick black hair without finding him, she realized he'd played the same game. After all, hadn't he been the one to teach it to her?

With a muffled curse, she forced herself to relax and walked into the bar, feeling Troy following close behind. He'd been quiet on the walk over, probably figuring silence would keep him from breaking down and talking her out of the meeting. She appreciated his holding back, as well as giving her time to think. Although she suspected no amount of time could prepare her for what Jim had in store.

Her step faltered when two familiar figures caught her attention. To the untrained eye, Daniel Chase and Brent Mason, Troy's fellow officers, would be difficult to miss because of their unique good looks and larger-than-life presence. To Ruby's ex-hustler way of viewing her surroundings, however, they simply screamed *cops.*

"What did you do?" Ruby whispered to Troy out of the side of her mouth.

Hand riding the small of her back, he sighed against her ear. "Please don't be angry. They care about you and—"

"And you wanted to give me a visible reminder of my new life. In case I forget."

He shook his head once. "I'm not going to deny that was part of it."

Ruby tipped her head back as if she'd find patience on the ceiling. "Troy, I hate that he knows about you. Hate it. I don't want him knowing our friends, too. You shouldn't have involved them."

"They're not involved." He pulled her closer. "I don't fuck around with your safety. He might be your father, but he's a criminal. Daniel and Brent are the best cops I know, next to myself. I asked them here because I want to be prepared for anything."

Brent spotted them then and gave Troy a barely perceptible nod. Noticing his friend's slight action, Daniel's beer froze halfway to his mouth, then continued its journey without acknowledging Ruby and Troy. "Wow. They've certainly been prepped. This might be the quietest I've ever seen Brent."

Troy's mouth twitched, but the humor didn't find his eyes. "No telling how long he'll last."

"Hopefully it'll be over quick enough that we won't have to find out. Let's go sit." Ruby blew out a breath and headed toward an empty four-seat table located in a dimmer section of the bar. "God, I just want to be home."

"Soon, baby."

Out of the corner of her eye, Ruby spotted Bowen Driscol sitting in the corner with his back propped against the brick wall. Baseball cap pulled down low on his forehead, he slowly nursed a bottle of beer. He kept his head down, his posture casual, but Ruby knew better. Her best friend since childhood kept himself ready to strike at any moment. Four years her senior, Bowen had been by her side those dangerous years she'd spent hustling men twice her age out of money. Countless times, he'd put himself between her and grave injury. Taking and giving beatings so she wouldn't have to. Then again earlier this year when she'd been caught trying to help incriminate Lenny, his crime boss father, he'd still remained unwaveringly loyal to her. Fathers who valued money over their children's safety was something they had in common.

Troy had called in her new friends for moral support and backup. She'd called Bowen. Ruby said a quick prayer, hoping Troy wouldn't spot him. He'd never understood the nature of their relationship. Didn't believe her that despite Bowen's good looks, charm, and overprotective attitude toward her, their rapport had always remained platonic. She'd always suspected Troy's dislike of Bowen stemmed from irrational guilt over not being around for Ruby those early years, and nothing she said seemed to dissuade him from his jealousy.

She hung her messenger bag over the back of her chair and sat. Troy took the chair beside her, creating a united front. Reaching over to take his hand, she tried not to stare at the door.

"Did you think I wouldn't see him?"

Ruby didn't pretend to misunderstand. "Please, don't read anything into it."

He continued as if she hadn't spoken. "What I can't decide is whether you lack faith in me, or—"

"No." Wide-eyed, she searched his closed-off expression. "It has nothing to do with faith. I trust you more than anyone, Troy." She racked her brain for a way to explain. "You wanted to remind me of my new life. Maybe I needed a reminder of the old one. But our goals were the same."

"If he's your past," Troy enunciated, "why won't he go away?"

"I don't want him to go away. I won't lose every part of myself to make you comfortable."

"You think I care about being comfortable?" Taken aback by his sudden fierce expression, she didn't answer. "I don't want to change a single damn thing about you. I just want you to myself."

"You have me. I'm yours. Don't ever question that."

His attention flickered as he brought his face close. "Keep right on looking at me. Your father just walked in." He brushed his mouth across hers. "Don't let him see you worried, baby."

Their argument faded immediately to the background, eclipsed by her sudden wave of gratefulness for Troy's presence. He was just as invested as she was in the upcoming encounter, and she would never be able to put into words how thankful she felt to have him there. It flooded her with confidence and reminded her that no matter how they fought, it always stemmed from love.

A chair scraped back at their table and she heard her father's deceptively smooth voice for the first time in years. "Hate to interrupt this heartwarming scene, but I'm on a time crunch."

Schooling her features, Ruby slowly faced her father. "No, you're not."

Jim Elliott tossed back his head and laughed. He hadn't aged a day. Not a single gray strand interrupted his stiff, slicked-back hair. His brown eyes were full of humor, but she could see the glint of danger lurking just beneath the surface. Hiding that lethal personality was one of his most valued traits. Her father had an uncanny ability to become your best friend while walking you off a cliff.

Jim threw an arm over the back of his chair and faced

them at an angle. Keeping his back turned from the entrance, she knew. The action drew her eye to the white cast on his wrist. To Jim, a visible injury equaled weakness, yet he wasn't hiding it. Her curiosity grew. "You can take the girl out of Brooklyn…" he murmured while signaling the waitress for a drink.

"Put it on our tab," Troy instructed the server when she took his order. *Bourbon, neat.*

"Oh, a *generous* cop. What a catch, Ru."

Her smile faltered at his use of her childhood nickname. She slipped her hand into Troy's strong grip. "He is a catch, thank you. If you came here just to insult us, we've got much better things to do."

Jim's fingers flexed on the table as he considered them. "What the hell is Driscol doing here?"

That gave Ruby a start. Until now, her father had shown no sign that he'd spotted Bowen lurking in the corner. Furthermore, she didn't understand Jim's hostility toward her friend. He had no reason to dislike him so intensely. "He's been looking out for me ever since you took off." She shrugged. "I guess old habits die hard."

"Looking out for you, huh?" Jim winked at Troy. "I bet you fucking love that."

Troy showed zero reaction. "Say what you came to say, Elliott. I'm getting impatient."

"You young people are all in such a rush nowadays." He smiled at the waitress as she dropped off his drink, blatantly checking out her ass when she turned around. "You know nothing about the art of anticipation."

Ruby almost laughed at the irony of that comment, but held her tongue. "If you need me to hustle for you, forget it. I've moved on."

He eyed her over his drink and her confidence dipped. "You haven't heard the stakes yet."

"No amount of money is worth getting tangled back up in your bullshit."

She couldn't tell if the flash of hurt on his face was manufactured or authentic, but the words had already been said and couldn't be taken back.

"You have your mother's uncanny ability to cut a man off at the knees." Jim nodded at Troy. "I bet she makes your life a balance of heaven and hell. Just like her mother did to me. Am I right?"

"Enough." Ruby jumped in before Troy could respond, her father's earlier comment ringing in her head. "My mother? You *never* talk about my mother."

"An oversight, perhaps." He lifted his shoulder and let it drop. "Tonight might be a good time to start talking about the elusive Pamela."

She felt Troy tense beside her, matching her own rigid posture. "What the hell is this?"

Jim pulled a notepad out of his jacket pocket and consulted it. Ruby knew he was just buying time. Heightening the anticipation, as he'd said. All an act. He never forgot a single detail. Which meant the mention of Pamela, her mother, hadn't been accidental. Dread welled in her gut. She'd been a mere child when her mother walked out, leaving her with her father, a man completely ill-equipped to raise her. For years, they'd traveled while Jim hustled and she slept in the backseat of their car or a dingy motel room. Until she'd learned to pull her own weight on the pool table. Never once, during all those years, did they speak about her mother.

Ruby looked over at Troy, silent communication passing between them. He anticipated something big on the horizon, too. She could see the anxiety on his face, though he tried valiantly to hide it.

Abruptly, Jim tossed the notepad on the table, apparently still trying to keep her off balance. Dammit, he would always be better at the game than she was. It was working. "The match will take place Tuesday night. Between you, should you agree, and a man named Robert Bell. We're still deciding on a location."

She frowned at the unfamiliar name. "Doesn't matter. I won't be there."

"I think you will." He tossed back his bourbon. "Robert Bell is your mother's brother. We're playing for information on her whereabouts. He has it. You win, and he hands her location over. I'd play the match myself, but..." He held up his injured right wrist.

Time froze. Nothing could have prepared her for this. Her father's words hit her like a roaring subway train, mowing her down in its path. She'd never allowed herself to wonder about the woman who'd abandoned them. There had never been a point. People didn't stick around in her world. Her old world, anyway. Yet now, the opportunity to find her mother glittered like gold in front of her eyes. Had it always been a subconscious desire she'd managed to smother?

Troy squeezed her hand hard enough to snap her back to the present. She sensed he wanted to drag her into his lap and rock her back and forth, but wouldn't allow her to lose face in front of her father. When he spoke, his voice was deadly silent. "What is Robert Bell's interest in this? What does he get if he wins?"

Jim chuckled as if the question had been absurd. "What else? Cash. Not to mention, his dislike of his sister rivals mine."

Troy obviously didn't buy it. "What's the catch, Elliott?"

"Catch?"

"Good question." Ruby finally cleared the rust from her throat. "Why now? What do you care where she is?"

Jim suddenly wouldn't meet her eyes, his fingers tracing moisture patterns on the table. "Look, I know I haven't been the best father to you, Ru. You're out of the game. I get it." His

Adam's apple bobbed in his throat. "I was wrong. Not telling you anything about her. You deserve to know. Let me give you this. You can consider it a parting gift if you want."

She sensed Bowen standing behind her, but didn't turn. Her attention was fixated solely on her father. He looked... contrite. Sincere. A rarity for Jim Elliott. God help her, she was affected by it. This *was* her father, after all. They'd been through good times and terrible times together. Sharing french fries on the hood of their car at a drive-in outside Pittsburgh. Sneaking into a Red Sox game in Boston, Jim sweet-talking them into seats along the first base line. Running through the rain to escape an angry bar owner for hustling his customers. They'd survived it all together. Could she believe him on this? She desperately wanted to, dammit. Finding out who her mother was, possibly having her questions answered, could finally be the closure stamp on her past.

Bowen finally spoke up, the barely leashed violence in his voice familiar to her. "Send her into a goddamn lion's den and call it a gift. Classic Jim Elliott."

"Watch it, Driscol." Her father wagged his finger and somehow made it look threatening. "Remember, I've got your number. Don't fuck with me."

Again, Ruby was taken aback by the friction between Bowen and Jim. The three of them hadn't spent a lot of time together in the past, Bowen having stepped in as her protector when Jim left town, but she didn't understand the antagonism there. She opened her mouth, ready to question it, when Troy's fist came down hard on the table. *Slam*. Out of the corner of her eye, Ruby saw Brent and Daniel ease back in their chairs, attempting to appear casual as they observed the situation closely.

"If you two want to have a pissing contest, do it on someone else's time," Troy ordered, shooting both men a look, before addressing her father alone. "You expect us to

believe you're doing this out of the goodness of your heart?
You think she's not smart enough to see right through you?"

"I don't know. Ask her." He challenged Ruby with a look
she remembered too well. "Or maybe she lets her big bad cop
boyfriend speak for her now."

Troy cursed. Bowen snorted. Ruby ignored them both,
feeling slightly resentful over their attempting to babysit her.
She could take care of herself. She'd done it for years. No, this
was *her* decision and the way she saw it, she didn't really have
a choice at all. It was very likely that Jim had an angle and
wasn't being honest. She could get up and walk away. Give up
the chance, dangerous or not, to find out about her mother.
Or, she could do what she did best. Hustle first, ask questions
later. In this case, didn't the reward justify the risk? *God hates
a coward, Ruby.*

She braced herself. "When will you know the location?"

Jim didn't look triumphant in the least, as if he'd been
expecting her agreement. "Soon."

"Ruby, you can't be serious." Troy turned in his seat, blue
eyes blazing. "It's obvious he's lying to you. Don't do this."

"The cop is right, Rubik's Cube," Bowen seconded grimly.
"You know I don't admit that easily."

"Shut it, Driscol."

Jim leaned back in his chair, folding his hands behind his
head. "Well, well. Now who's having the pissing contest?" His
countenance went hard. "She's made her decision. Live with
it, boys."

Ruby pushed back her chair and stood, so Jim was forced
to look up at her. He narrowed his eyes at the power move.
"Let's get one thing straight, Jim. I know there's something
you're not telling me. You're a con and I doubt you ever saw
me as anything but a meal ticket. I'm agreeing because I'm
curious. That's the *only* reason. Not because I believe your
sob story about some misplaced sense of guilt. Nice try,

though, *Father.*"

Troy moved behind her, placing a hand on the small of her back as they walked out of Quincy's, Bowen sauntering a few steps behind. They were still supporting her even though she'd probably just disappointed them both. She brushed a hand down Troy's arm, letting him know she appreciated his keeping himself in check. Although Ruby knew, without a doubt, he wouldn't give a damn about her saving face once they got home.

Chapter Four

Troy made a concerted effort not to break something, even though in his current state of mind, every inanimate object in their apartment looked like a perfect target for his fist. Goddammit, he felt helpless. It was an unfamiliar feeling for him and he didn't handle it well. He'd known going into this relationship with Ruby that she was a wild card. Her penchant for trouble and unwillingness to see disasters in her path were traits he'd had to accept in order to keep her. Troy didn't regret his decision for a moment, and never would. His love for Ruby intensified by the day. She consumed him. She was his life. And when he said all those months ago that he wasn't budging, he fucking meant it. But right now, when that deep-seated fear of losing someone he loved came roaring to the surface, he wondered at his own sanity.

Last year, after losing his partner in a gun battle, meeting Ruby had been a cruel twist of fate. His vow to play it safe had been buried by his hot, clamoring need to have her. He'd never had a chance. Nor had that need even remotely faded.

He thought they'd graduated to a place where compromise

had become natural. That at the very least, they would consider each other before barreling headlong into danger. Yet once again, she'd put herself in a potentially unsafe situation, without giving a thought to how it affected him. Just envisioning her in some seedy pool hall, surrounded by a dozen low-life Soprano wannabes, in all likelihood carrying weapons, made him break out in a cold sweat. Without hesitation, he would protect her with his life. But he didn't like variables. He only dealt in certainties when it came to Ruby.

Troy watched as she removed her coat and hung it on the back of a chair. Her movements were slow, resigned, as if she'd reconciled herself to the upcoming argument. It pissed him off even more, her apparent belief that she could predict him so well. *We'll see about that, baby.* She expected a lecture. She thought he would beg for the right to protect her? *Fuck. That.* He'd already earned the right. No discussion required.

He tossed his keys on the dining room table on his way down the hallway, stripping his shirt over his head as he went. "I'm turning in."

She walked into their bedroom a moment later as he kicked off his shoes. "Troy?"

Something sharp moved in his chest at the smallness in her voice. With determination, he blocked the need to hold her. "Yeah."

"Are you all right?"

"No. I'm not all right, Ruby. Did you think I would be?"

She shook her head, dark hair fanning out at her shoulders. "Why aren't you saying anything? Why aren't you telling me how reckless I'm being?"

"It never does me any good."

"Stop being so cold," she demanded. "I don't like it. This isn't you."

"You don't like it…" He trailed off with a laugh. She'd just cut the tenuous thread of faith he'd been holding on to and she expected him to be his usual supportive self? Impossible. He was free-falling into full-scale panic. *Ruby in danger. Again.* "I don't like showing up to Quincy's and seeing Driscol there, not knowing what the fuck he means to you. I don't like sitting there listening to your father plot your next deadly adventure and keeping my mouth shut. Being so damn sure I can trust you to make the right call. And being wrong."

She jerked back a little, making him wish for a split second that he hadn't been so harsh. "You don't understand."

"Actually, I think I'm finally starting to understand. You don't miss that lifestyle after all." He unbuckled his jeans, kicked them off. "It's like a bad movie. Just one last score. Only it's never the last time. It never will be."

Her brown eyes lit with anger then, her temper only making her more beautiful. Troy watched her in awe, pressure building in his chest. *God, I love her. Happy. Livid. Any way and every way.*

"Look at you on your fucking high horse, Troy Bennett. You think I'm doing this for some kind of cheap thrill?" She stomped toward him and pushed against his bare chest. He pressed into her hands, his body, as always, craving any form of contact with hers. "You've got your big happy family, your bosomy mother. You grew up in a perfect neighborhood, slept in a bed with clean sheets. What the hell do you know about being abandoned? About wondering if you did something wrong to send them away?"

Troy's anger, along with his heart, sank like lead into his stomach. Jesus, no. Had he made a massive error here? After leaving Quincy's, he'd been so caught up in his own pissed-off mental state, his own worry, that he'd completely glossed over the bombshell that had been dropped on her tonight. *Fucking idiot.* When she went to shove at his chest again, he grabbed her wrists and tried to bring her close, but she resisted. "Baby, I'm sorry—"

"Too late." She yanked her hands away. "All this worry over something happening to me, it's all because you're so damn scared to feel an ounce of anything negative. Well, that's all I felt for years. So deal with it, Troy. Okay? Life isn't always sunshine and roses."

"Of course I fucking worry." His voice rose to match hers. "I can't cut that part out of myself any more than I can stop loving you—"

"But you would if you could," she cut in, her voice sounding suddenly numb. "You'd stop loving me in a heartbeat if it was possible. Just to save yourself from any potential pain or loss." Her laughter fell on his ears like stones. "My father was right, wasn't he? I am your heaven and hell."

Troy could no longer stem the rising tide of panic. There was not a hint of his Ruby behind her eyes. This conversation, the entire night, had gotten away from him in a way he'd never thought possible. He'd actually forced her to question his feelings? How was such a thing possible, when he needed her just to survive? She was his life. He thought he'd left no room for her to doubt that. With firm hands, he gripped her forearms. This time she didn't protest, but looked up at him defiantly. "Listen to me. Don't let this, don't let *him*, come between us." He shook her gently. "I wouldn't stop loving you, Ruby, if it meant the end to everything else I know, love, or care about in this world. As long as I had you, I'd be all right."

A tear rolled down her cheek, devastating him. "God, I-I can't think around you. I've got so much to process, so much to think about, and you take up all the air." She dragged in a labored breath. "I'm going to Hayden's. I just need a night away."

A knife in his chest. "No."

"You can't tell me no."

Troy's hand went to the hem of her shirt and slipped beneath, as if he had no control over it. His last resort was taking over, trying to keep her with him at all costs. Her skin felt like warm silk under his fingers as they teased her belly, drifted lower. "Stay. Let me ease you here, baby. I'm nowhere without you...just let me bring you back." Their hips connected and he rolled his body against her. "Let me go so deep that we forget everything. You know I'm hard. I'm always hard."

"Stop," she moaned. "Not like this."

Trying to ignore the painful ache her words afflicted him with, he tilted her head to the side so he could suck at her neck. "What's wrong, baby? You want to be on top?" He sank his teeth into the flesh beneath her ear. "You know I go fucking crazy when you ride me. I love watching you pretend to be in charge when we both know I could have you under me, screaming for God in one damn move."

Ruby's legs squeezed together and she whimpered, telling him he had her. He could lever her against the wall and fuck her for an hour straight, both of them loving every pulse-pounding minute. But the sound was layered with sadness. Disappointment. In him? Herself? No, he wouldn't take the damage he'd done tonight and make it worse. Even if he wanted her with a desperation that shook him to his soul. With incredible difficulty, he stepped away. She dipped a little, her knees buckling, but he held her upright by his grip on her arms.

"Troy...I want you, but it hurts," she panted, her hand rubbing at her chest. "It shouldn't hurt."

"Go." His voice sounded hoarse. "Go before I change my mind."

She studied him for a moment. "It's just tonight. I need some space. Don't overthink it."

Troy nodded dumbly, watching in a dreamlike state, as the girl he loved walked out on him.

• • •

Brent opened the front door to the house he shared with his wife, Hayden, before Ruby even rang the bell. She had to crane her neck to look up at him, the NYPD explosives expert was so damn tall. Knowing she probably looked terrible, since she was treading in the emotional wreckage of the last few hours, Ruby rubbed the sleeve of her jacket under her eyes and laughed uncomfortably.

"Sorry. It's not even Halloween and you've got something scary on your doorstep." She gestured to her mascara-stained cheeks. "Not suitable for male company, big guy."

Brent gave her a sympathetic smile and patted her on the back. "Hey, I've got a sister, a sister-in-law, two nieces, twin baby girls, and a high-maintenance wife. As long as it's not directed at me, you can cry me a river, sweetheart."

Hayden appeared behind him rolling her eyes, obviously having overheard her husband's attempt to comfort, but Ruby glimpsed the underlying affection there. "It's *usually* directed at him. Come in, Ruby. Story is on her way over with sangria."

"And that's my cue to head over to the town house," Brent said, referring to Hayden's posh ex-residence, the one she'd lived in before they married, but still kept for convenience. He snatched his duffel bag off the floor of the foyer. "I seriously doubt Daniel and Troy would appreciate me being the only rooster at this hen party."

Hayden stood on her toes to give Brent a kiss. "See ya, Flo."

"'Night, Duchess." He winked at her. "If you ladies burn your bras, I want photographic evidence." His attention transferred to Ruby. "Hey, whatever happened tonight, I know it was tough. But you and Troy are tougher. Capiche?"

"Capiche," Ruby mumbled, trading places with him in the doorway. She walked into the house toward Hayden's living room, hoping to give the couple another minute together. Part of her felt like shit for interrupting their night together—*again*—since Brent had already been at Quincy's on her behalf, but mostly, she was too drained to process guilt. She dropped her purse onto the couch and plunked down next to it, observing the newly decorated interior with weary eyes. Baby toys, bouncy chairs, pink quilts. Although it was far from the first time she'd been in Hayden and Brent's babyproofed home, after the events of the night and having her past dangled in front of her face, she felt even more out of place than usual. Upon meeting Hayden months ago, she'd been positive the class divide would eliminate the possibility of friendship. What did a girl who lived over a noodle shop in Brooklyn and an Upper West Side debutante have in common?

Shockingly, their differences had never entered into the equation. While Hayden radiated confidence, the more time Ruby spent with her, it became apparent that she didn't always know where she fit in among her peers, either. They'd connected on that level, and Ruby's doubts about finding common ground with a rich girl had been sunk. Now, however, staring her friend's newfound matrimonial bliss and parenthood in the eye, she'd never felt further from connected to anyone. Anything. Had she ever had a single baby toy or quilt? She couldn't even remember.

Hayden strode into the living room then, her steps brisk and efficient. She jerked a thumb over her shoulder. "Look what I found outside."

Story, Daniel Chase's wife, followed close behind, flip-flops slapping on the wood floor, a pitcher of sangria held aloft. "I come bearing gifts of great honor."

Ruby smiled. "Where are the other two wise men?"

"Their camels are in the shop."

"Holding a glass pitcher of alcohol and wearing flip-flops in this cold-ass weather." Hayden shook her head sadly. "How the hell did you get a cab to stop for you?"

Story shrugged. "I offered some sangria to the driver."

Hayden exchanged a glance with Ruby. "Offering alcohol to your driver. So many things wrong with that, I don't even know where to start." She poured the red liquid into three glasses she'd retrieved from the kitchen. "But my babies are finally sleeping, so let's just drink."

"Amen," Ruby agreed. "Thanks for this, guys. I know it's late."

"Bah."

"Meh."

"I know you're probably wondering what happened. I'll get around to it." Ruby took a healthy sip of her drink. "Mind talking about something else for a while first?"

"Sure. I'll go." Story knelt in front of the coffee table, leaned forward on her elbows. "My mom is in town, spending time with Daniel Junior." Her eyes sparkled at the mention of her newborn son. "We had dinner with my father. Daniel charmed the living crap out of everyone, as usual." Her eyes squeezed shut. "But afterward, I'm pretty sure my mother and my father…I think they…"

"Fucked?"

"Hayden! Oh my God." Story drained her glass of sangria in one gulp. "Not okay."

Ruby bit her lip to keep from laughing. "What tipped you off? No pun intended."

"Screw you both." Story composed herself. "The next morning, they met us in the park. We were planning on checking out that exhibit at MOMA. You know the one. With that actress who's sleeping in the glass box for a week?"

Hayden nodded once. "Yeah. Art."

"Right. I think." Story shook her head as if to clear it. "Anyway, I saw them get out of a cab together. Jack might have…well, he pinched my mom's ass. Jesus, I'm going to vomit."

Without missing a beat, Ruby dumped a bucket of toy blocks on the rug and handed Story the container.

"Hey!" Hayden protested. "My children play with that— oh, fuck it. There's already puke everywhere." She joined Story on the carpet. "So your parents took a little stroll down memory lane. What's the big deal?"

Story groaned. "That's what Daniel said."

"He's right. A little nooky for old time's sake. No harm in it."

"Speaking of parents," Ruby blurted. "My father arranged a pool match for me. Against my uncle, who I've never met, but I'm pretty sure is a criminal. If I win, they'll tell me where my mother is. She bailed when I was in diapers. I can't even remember her face." She took a deep breath. "I said yes. Troy is pissed as hell over me agreeing to the match. Not to mention, Bowen being there tonight." Her head started to pound. "Also, I just walked out on him while he was trying to seduce me."

She looked up from her rambling speech to find her friends wide-eyed, glasses of sangria frozen halfway to their mouths.

Story cleared her throat. "Okay, so my parents fucked. No big deal."

Hayden set her drink down carefully and looked at Ruby. "All right, let's take this apart piece by piece. First off, if you don't mind me asking about Bowen...?"

"Nothing there. *Ever.* He's my best friend." She massaged her forehead. "At least, he was before Troy. Now everything is so damn confusing."

"What's your father's motivation for doing this?" Ruby noted that Story, usually carefree and full of easy laughter, had turned serious. She knew from past conversations that Story had studied hostage negotiation as a child to feel closer to her father, the legendary negotiator Jack Brooks. Hence, the technical question that seemed so out of place coming from the sunny blonde.

"That's the issue. Jim has never done anything in his life unless he benefited on the other side. Troy thinks there's more to the story." Her throat felt tight just saying his name. What was he doing right now? "I don't disagree with him, but I can't walk away without trying. It's my mother. I've taken bigger risks for far less reward."

"I understand. Wanting to find your mother." Hayden looked far off for a moment. "Troy will, too. He probably just needs some time."

"He'll find a way to make it safe," Story added.

"Right. Safe." Ruby blew out a breath. "While he's so busy risking his neck to keep me protected, who's going to watch out for him?"

Chapter Five

Troy didn't look up when three shadows darkened his desk the next morning.

"Heads up, Bennett. Your princes have arrived." Brent.

"Is he ignoring us?" Daniel.

"Looks that way." And fuck, they'd brought Matt along. Known among them as the Relationship Whisperer. The ex–military sniper rarely spoke, but when he decided to grace them with his patient philosophical observations, it tended to knock a man on his ass. The truth could do that. As if he hadn't been Yoda-esque before, ever since he'd married Brent's younger sister, Lucy, his penchant for telling the truth had only increased tenfold. Troy had been subjected to more than enough truth for one twenty-four-hour period, so he held up his middle finger hoping they'd all take the hint and leave him the hell alone.

"Maybe later. If Hayden says it's okay," Brent responded jovially to his silent *fuck you.*

Daniel sighed, shooting Brent a look. "Start talking, Troy, or we'll sic Matt on you."

Troy punched a series of codes into his computer to get him into the department database. "Matt, what did they promise you in exchange for sitting through this?"

"Two days free of them oversharing about their wives. And an indefinite hiatus from hearing every single detail of their children's sleeping and eating schedules."

Like him and Ruby, Matt and Lucy weren't quite as ready to dive into diaper duty as their friends. They seemed more than happy to bask in their newlywed status for the moment.

"Look, I'm going to get the story out of my wife sooner or later," Daniel tried again, ignoring Matt's deadpan explanation. "She's ticklish."

Matt sipped his mug of coffee. "And hiatus over."

Troy leaned back in his chair, massaging the bridge of his nose. "Ruby's father wants her to play one last match against her lowlife uncle. She wins, uncle hands over her long-gone, deadbeat mother's whereabouts."

Daniel's eyes narrowed. "What's the catch?"

"Exactly. He swears it's a parting gift. An apology for not being father of the year."

"Bullshit," Brent said.

Matt set his mug down carefully. "But you're pissed, so I'm assuming Ruby accepted the match."

Troy confirmed with a nod.

"Shit," all three men said at the same time.

A moment of silence passed, broken by Daniel clearing his throat. "Look, I'm not saying she should have accepted the risk, but I understand. Wanting to know your mother and where you came from."

Troy absorbed that, but since he'd already spent the night mentally berating himself for not understanding Ruby's decision, it made little difference. Daniel had been a foster child, so of course it made immediate sense to him, proving her words from last night correct. Thanks to his ideal upbringing, he wasn't able to fully comprehend her decision.

Matt zeroed in on Daniel, picking up on the subtlest of undercurrents as usual. "The way you said that...have you looked into *your* birth parents?"

Daniel didn't appear surprised at Matt's question. They were never surprised anymore when he picked up on something they thought well-hidden. "Yeah. I mean, just preliminary stuff. Filing papers...reaching out, I guess you would say."

"Does Story know?" Troy asked.

"Not yet," Daniel answered, looking contrite. "I don't want her getting her hopes up for me. You know how she is." He shrugged. "It never mattered before...who my parents were. But I want to know everything now. Medical history, especially. We've got our son to think about now. Hopefully another son or daughter somewhere down the road." Daniel cleared his throat. "Okay, *now*. I basically can't get Story pregnant fast enough."

Brent looked smug. "Someone is jealous of my twins."

"None of you say a damn thing to her," Daniel warned while shooting Brent the bird. "I just bought her a puppy to ease her into the idea of more kids."

"What kind of puppy did you get?" Brent crossed his arms over his barrel-sized chest. "It better not be one of those bullshit Chihuahuas, bro. I'll lose all respect for you."

"Oh, did I actually have your respect at some point?"

Matt's loud exhale quieted the pair. "Can we get back to the problem at hand? Not that this domestic detour hasn't been riveting."

"I've already explained the problem." Troy plucked a handful of papers from his printer, laying them on the desk. "And I've been working on the solution. Ruby isn't in possession of her birth certificate. But last night Jim mentioned the uncle, Robert Bell. I'm working on narrowing it down by finding him, then searching for siblings. Problem is, the name Robert Bell is so goddamn common."

"You're trying to find her mother before the match," Matt deduced. "So it won't be necessary."

"Right."

Daniel took one of the printouts. "Jesus. Hundreds in New York and New Jersey alone. Let's split it up three ways. We'll take turns putting surveillance on Jim Elliott. He could end up leading us to the guy's doorstep."

"No. I didn't ask for your help." Troy shook his head determinedly. "This isn't an official investigation and I'm not dragging you guys into it. You've got your own shit going on."

"True." Brent snatched up his own list. "But nothing to prevent us from keeping Ruby safe. If you recall, she put her ass on the line for us once," he reminded them, referring to the reckless move she'd made to protect Troy, placing herself at risk to locate their suspect's whereabouts. A situation eerily similar to the last twenty-four hours. "I'd like to return the favor."

"Don't ever mention her ass again. Or returning the favor."

Brent winked. "Message received, Mr. Sensitive."

When Brent and Daniel walked away, still arguing over dog breeds, Matt nudged the remaining list in Troy's direction. "I'll take the first shift on Elliott. You should go see Ruby and get your head straight. Not the wisest move going searching for her father when the two of you are arguing. You could end up doing something you regret."

"She left." Troy pretended to be engrossed in something on his computer screen. "She hasn't done that since our first week together."

"She's scared. People who are used to fear...sometimes they would rather exist inside that fear without the benefit of comfort. It's a familiar place and it gives them an excuse to alienate the people closest to them. To rely solely on themselves." He looked across the bustling station. "She probably feels worse than you do for leaving. Go see her."

"I will." He thought of her tear-heavy eyes as she'd left their apartment last night. Pushing too soon could push her away. "When it's time."

. . .

Ruby left the workshop just as the sun started to set, beginning her twenty-minute trek across town to get home. Something stopped her at the subway entrance, when she normally would have walked right past. Fingers curled around the strap of her messenger bag, she stood watching rush-hour commuters descend the stairs leading underground, on their way to Brooklyn. She wasn't ready to go home to Troy on the Upper East Side just yet. Their argument the night before still felt fresh, and frankly, she'd been too busy today to sort through her emotions. Or maybe she'd just been avoiding them. Either way, she needed more time.

Without giving herself a chance to reconsider, she joined the moving mass of people, swiped her MetroCard, and boarded the train toward her old neighborhood. The routine felt so familiar, yet incredibly different. Looking at her reflection in the sliding doors, she realized how much she'd changed. No pool stick strapped to her back. The trademark belligerent expression that had defined her seemed to have faded, too. She'd changed for the better, but she suspected if emotional baggage were a visible trait, it would still sit squarely on her shoulders.

When the train pulled into the Grand Army Plaza stop, she ducked under the arms of passengers holding on to the overhead bar for balance and stepped into the bustling station. A few short minutes later, she found herself across the street from her old apartment above the noodle shop. She must have been subconsciously heading there, but couldn't decide why. Perhaps she needed a reminder of how far she'd come, remind herself what was at stake. Maybe she just needed to be somewhere familiar, to ground herself now that everything was spinning out of control again.

"You must be lost." Another familiar voice. "The Upper East Side is back that way. Just follow the trail of Pilates instructors and Botox needles."

She laughed for the first time that day. "What are you doing here, Bowen?"

"Some of us still live here, Rhubarb Pie."

"Right." As if on cue, they both leaned back against the stacks of newspapers on display outside the bodega. Ruby looked back across the street at her first permanent home, but she could feel Bowen's eyes on her. "What?"

He took off his ball cap, ran a hand through his mane of dark blond hair, and replaced it. "Troy know you're out here?"

"I don't want to talk about him right now."

"That's a no."

Ruby sighed. There was a time when she told Bowen everything, but it didn't feel right talking to him about Troy. It would feel like a betrayal of confidence, especially when Troy had never felt comfortable with them spending time together. "So are you going to give me shit about accepting the match, too? That's not why I came out here."

"Why *did* you come here?"

"Hell if I know." They laughed silently until Ruby grew serious once more. "You know what it's like…growing up without a mom. Wouldn't you jump at the chance to find out?"

Bowen shifted and looked away. "I don't know. Where we come from, some things are better left staying a secret."

"Curiosity killed the cat?"

He hummed in his throat. "Look, I know you're getting it

from all sides, so I'm only going to say this once." His warm hand, knuckles covered in bruises, lay down on top of hers. "Don't do it. If you agreed just to be stubborn, to show your father you're not scared, swallow that pride and back out."

She ripped her hand from beneath his. "You think you know me so damn well?" Even as she asked the question, she knew it was absurd. He knew her better than almost anyone.

A flicker of insecurity crossed his features. "Maybe not anymore. But I know all about how pointless it is trying to impress a father. They're numb, Ruby. They don't feel a goddamn thing."

His words felt like a blow. "That's not what this is about."

"Fine." He pulled a pack of cigarettes out of his pocket and tapped one into his hand. "Subject closed."

Ruby struggled to put out a flicker of guilt, but didn't want to dwell on the subject. Her mind was made up. "How are things going for you here? With your father away."

He took his time lighting the cigarette, then met her eyes, smoke curling around his lips. "Bad."

A pit formed in her stomach. "Are you…running things now?" Bowen didn't answer her, just continued blowing streams of smoke into the cool evening air, all but confirming her suspicion. Her actions of last year had helped the NYPD put Lenny Driscol, Bowen's father and South Brooklyn's notorious mob boss, behind bars on numerous charges, including her own attempted murder. Obviously, Bowen had been a victim of the fallout. *Oh God, no.* "I-is there anything I can do to help?"

Bowen shook his head. "Just can't stay out of trouble, can you?" He threw an arm around her shoulders, pulled her up against his side. "I don't know why we worry about each other at all," he said on an exhale. "We're survivors. We'll just keep coming back for more."

Ruby started to press, to tell him for the hundredth time

that if they worked together, they could pull him out of the lifestyle, but something caught her eye. A police car pulled to a stop across the street. Not an unusual occurrence in this neighborhood, but she'd recognize the silhouette of the driver anywhere. Without thinking, she pulled away from Bowen, just as Troy exited the vehicle and slammed the door behind him.

Even in the near-darkness, she could see his features were tight, his fists bunched at his sides as he crossed the street. On autopilot, she stood and moved in front of Bowen.

"Don't even think about fighting with him," she warned him over her shoulder.

"If he calls me out, Ruby, there's nothing I can do about it."

She cursed. "Troy—"

"Get out of the way."

Ruby pressed a hand to his hard chest, feeling a frisson of alarm at the cold expression on his face. "You need to stop and listen."

Troy completely ignored her. "Let's go, Driscol. Unless you're planning on hiding behind her all night."

Bowen immediately skirted past her, stripping off his jacket. "Sorry, Ruby. Tried my best. Is he left-handed or right?"

Christ, the jerk sounded almost chipper. "Stop this, now." Keeping her hold on Troy, she tried to push Bowen back. "Troy, we were just talking. You're being—"

"I'm being *what*?" His attention snapped to her. Words failed her in the face of his anger. "Jealous? I've never pretended otherwise. I've never been even remotely okay with this and I just found you glued together on the street corner." He shook his head. "You had to know this was inevitable."

"He's right," Bowen piped up behind her. "Let him get his shot at me. I've been wondering if he can protect you as well as he claims." He tossed his ball cap on the pavement.

"Time to find out."

Teeth bared, Troy yanked her hand off his chest and pulled her behind his back. "Don't interfere."

Ruby lifted her hands and let them fall. "You know what? Go ahead and beat each other to a bloody pulp. Maybe it'll dislodge your heads from your asses."

There was no stopping it, she realized in a daze. The moment Troy reached her best friend, he reared back with a right hook and blasted Bowen square in the jaw. Bowen, looking momentarily stunned, staggered back, then lunged forward to tackle Troy down to the pavement where they traded a series of punches. They exchanged the upper hand several times as people gathered on the sidewalk to watch the fight, a couple of neighborhood lifers even nodding as if impressed. Ruby had never seen Troy fight, but Bowen, a street fighter since his early teens, had clearly met his match. Troy was relentless, never pausing in his assault, even as Bowen battled back. When she saw blood trickling into Bowen's eye from a nasty cut, she forced herself between them. With his vision obscured, it would no longer be fair and she was tired of people being hurt because of her. She shoved with all her might to break them apart. Both of them backed off a little, presumably afraid they might accidentally hit her.

"That's enough, Troy. You've made your point."

Bowen swiped a hand across his mouth and laughed when he saw blood. "No one's made me bleed in a while. Not bad. You're still an asshole."

Troy licked his split lip. "I'll do worse if you ever touch her again."

Ruby's temper finally went through the roof. In that moment, it felt as though she'd lost her hard-won independence. These two men, whom she admittedly loved in very different ways, thought they could control her actions. They thought she needed protecting from herself, from everything. And she'd had enough. She was tired of having her judgment questioned.

"Well, I'm glad you two shitheads feel better." She backed away from them slowly. "But I, for one, am done here."

Troy's expression turned wary. "What does that mean?"

"I don't know. I just can't look at you right now."

"Ruby, listen—"

"I should listen to *you* now?" Her voice was incredulous. "After you completely ignored me and went straight for my best friend's throat?" She suddenly couldn't care less who was within earshot, the words spilling from her mouth in a choked whisper. "You're taking the control I give you in bed and letting it spread too far. Rein it in or we're done."

"Way more than I needed to hear," Bowen grumbled behind her.

Troy's eyebrows had risen at her words.

"What?" Her throat felt tight, tears burning behind her eyes. She interpreted the surprise on his face to mean only one thing. He didn't trust her around Bowen. Possibly never had. "Does it surprise you that I would mention our sex life in front of Bowen? Why?"

He took a step toward her, eyes narrowed as if trying to discern her point. "Let's go home and talk. I don't think we're on the same page."

Her laughter sounded slightly hysterical. "I'm not going anywhere with you."

A flare of alarm crossed his features. "You said one night. One."

"Well, I changed my damn mind." She split a look between them. "I can do that. I'm allowed. I'm also allowed to tell you both to back off. Thank you for your concern, but I don't need protecting every moment of every day. You do me a disservice by acting otherwise."

Bowen shifted on his feet. "Jesus, Ruby—"

"Why were you really here, Bowen? You live two stops away." She blurted before the realization had fully formed, "Were you following me?"

He stayed silent a moment. "Look, I'm sorry. With Jim around…"

"And you?" Without waiting for him to finish, she transferred her irritation to Troy. "Just happened to be in the neighborhood?"

Troy said nothing, but she saw the answer in his eyes. Just like always, he'd taken matters into his own hands without consulting her. She'd seen it coming, but it still rankled. Without another word, she spun on her heel and headed toward the subway at a fast clip. Before she could descend the stairs, Troy grabbed her arm, slowing her.

"You shut me out. I didn't have a choice."

"Me either, apparently." She pulled her arm free. "I won't live my life under surveillance."

He stared at her hard, conflict written all over his features. "I can't take the chance."

"Even if it means losing me?"

"Don't say that," he grated, voice shaking with intensity.

Troy tried to pull her close, but she evaded him. "Answer me. Will you insist on treating me like I'm breakable even if it means losing me?"

His head fell forward on a weary sigh. "If it comes down to a choice between your safety, your *life*, and keeping you as my girlfriend, I'd keep you safe every time. I'm sorry. It's how I'm built, Ruby."

Ruby swiped at the tear rolling down her cheek. "What about how I'm built?" She didn't wait for him to answer, but turned and descended into the station, feeling Troy's hard gaze on her back until she disappeared from view.

Chapter Six

Troy stood on the sidewalk outside Ruby's workshop, wondering at the reception he was going to get inside. It had been two days since his fight with Bowen in Brooklyn and their subsequent confrontation. Two miserable days wherein he'd kept as much distance as he could. Letting them both cool down. He'd spent the time working around the clock, tracking down her uncle, Robert Bell, in New Jersey. From that point, he'd thought it would be smooth sailing. Find Bell's sister, also known as Ruby's mother, and avoid the upcoming match. Unfortunately, Pamela Bell had virtually dropped off the face of the earth over two decades ago. He'd searched for Pamela Elliott, too, in case she'd married Jim at some point and Ruby hadn't been made aware of the union. Nothing.

With the clock ticking down and none of his work panning out, he'd finally left his desk. He'd needed to clear his head, find a different angle to work. Before he knew it, he'd found himself here. Knowing she was on the other side of the door was making him crazy. They hadn't spent a single night apart since their first week together, and it was starting to take its toll on him. Whether it led to an argument or something beneficial, he needed to see her. God willing, she'd let him touch her. He needed that connection. Their relationship transcended the physical, but he wouldn't deny that sex with Ruby grounded him. Right now, when he felt frustrated, helpless to repair any of the problems on his plate, he needed her with startling intensity.

Yet as badly as he desired Ruby, he wouldn't lay a finger on her unless she initiated. The first night she'd left, asking for space, he'd tried to use their mutual attraction against her. Inexcusable. Then he'd made the situation infinitely worse by going to battle with Driscol in the middle of an intersection. He didn't regret the fight. No, it had felt too damn good. But afterward, hearing the pain in Ruby's voice when she questioned his trust…that had been unbearable.

Now that he'd gotten some distance, he could easily see how she'd drawn the false conclusion that he didn't trust her, when he did with his whole heart. She was the most loyal person he knew, by a mile. That didn't mean he could stomach the sight of another man comforting her, the night after he'd failed to do just that. He'd reacted out of self-disgust on top of jealousy. Two days passing without an opportunity to apologize or explain had been his punishment.

If he'd just stopped to explain his position to her sooner, this argument could have been avoided. When you loved someone as much as he loved Ruby, it was impossible to imagine someone, namely Bowen, spending five minutes in her presence and not feeling the same way. It was why he'd never been able to reconcile their friendship. Not completely.

Without giving himself a chance to further question his decision to come, Troy walked into Ruby's workshop, the smell of sawdust and teak oil permeating the air. He loved coming here, seeing her current projects. Watching her speak on the phone with such confidence and authority. Today, however, he didn't know what to expect. White paper bags balanced in his hand, Troy came to a stop in front of Mya's desk. She jumped a little at his presence, the blaring death metal having drowned out his approaching footsteps.

"Troy. Jesus, there goes ten years off my already rapidly dwindling lifespan."

"Sorry, Mya." He handed her one of the bags. "Brought you a slice of pizza."

"All's forgiven."

"Is she here?"

Mya's gaze flickered. "Y-yes." She hesitated.

Troy looked past her to the stockroom. "But you're not sure she wants to see me."

"She hasn't really been herself this week." Mya shrugged one shoulder. "I figured you two must have gotten into it—"

"Mya, is someone here?" Ruby walked out of the stockroom then.

And turned Troy inside out.

In a short, tight black dress, she looked like forbidden sex on legs. The snug hem sat just a single devastating inch above the midway point of her thighs, revealing the skin she usually kept hidden in public underneath jeans. Jesus, if she were to stand in front of him, he'd only be required to nudge her panties to the side, dip his hips, and he'd be inside her in one hard upward thrust. Black suede knee-high boots completed the outfit, turning the dress from sexy to downright naughty. Her breasts, high and round, were braless and ready to bounce into his hands as soon as he tugged down the material to reveal them. Her pouty little nipples were outlined behind the thin material, making his palms itch to touch. His mouth watered, starved for a taste.

Any other day, he wouldn't hesitate to back her into the stockroom and ring her fucking bell. She'd love it, too. Ruby loved it when he couldn't control himself, because it was so rare. Control defined him. The fantasies playing themselves out in his head began causing him physical discomfort then, because he'd made up his mind not to touch her. Not unless *she* wanted it. He'd tried to use their intense sexual connection against her the other night. It sickened him that he'd taken something so pure and tainted it. As much as it killed him, he needed to walk away now. He couldn't have her, no matter how badly he needed to sink deep inside and reassure himself that no matter what differences lay between them, she craved him just as much as he craved her. No. If he took her now, when he risked losing control, she could slip even further from his reach. When he inevitably tried to control her, she'd take it as a sign that he still didn't understand her need for independence. "I brought you lunch." He set the bag down on Mya's desk. "You look beautiful today, baby."

Cursing once under his breath, he turned to walk out the door, still seeing her image in his mind's eye. Knowing he was doing the right thing did nothing to ease his blistering arousal.

"Troy." Ruby's voice behind him made his spine stiffen. He looked back over his shoulder to find her staring after him, a mixture of confusion and longing on her face, completely disarming him. They stayed that way for long moments before Mya cleared her throat in the sudden silence.

"I'm going to go grab some lunch." She rounded the desk, booted heels scuffing along the floor. "Be back in an hour."

"Okay, Mya."

When the door closed, neither of them moved. Troy could tell she was waiting for him to say something. Explain his odd behavior. "I came down here to talk, but now…" He shook his head. "It's impossible be this close and not hold you."

She took a few hesitant steps in his direction. A little closer and he could reach her. "Maybe I want to be held."

• • •

"Maybe?"

Ruby's pulse pounded loudly in her ears. She absorbed Troy's image greedily, reacquainting herself with the broad lines of his shoulders, the clearly defined muscles underneath his uniform shirt. The last two mornings, she'd woken with a powerful ache pulsing inside her, the one Troy was usually all too eager to satisfy. Her anger with him still existed in spades, but it did nothing to dull the insistent, consuming need. She'd kept it in check until now. Seeing him here, looking so tortured and frustrated…it was like looking in a mirror. Her body pleaded for relief. Pleaded for *his* relief, too. In her ears, the echo of her own shallow breathing sounded rhythmic, erotic.

"Just because we're in a bad place, doesn't mean I stop wanting you."

"I want you, too." His voice sounded harsher than moments before. "But I won't make this worse. No matter how difficult you're making it to walk away right now."

Ruby's heart tugged painfully at his honesty. They should talk. Straighten out the mess between them. Some stubborn part of her wasn't ready to do that, however. So instead, she closed the distance between them in a slow, sensual walk that elicited a deep growl from his throat. She felt her thighs flexing with each step and watched Troy's eyes linger there, rise to her gently swaying hips. His fists clenched and unclenched at his sides, as if desperate to touch her. Good. She was desperate to be touched.

When she finally reached him, she glided her hands over his hard chest. "How could it make things worse when we'll feel so much better afterward?"

He gripped her hips and groaned. "You're not playing fair, hustler."

Ruby went up on her toes to kiss his neck, smiling to herself when he tilted his head to make room for her mouth. "Are we going to play, Troy?" She dragged her curves over the rigid muscle of his stomach and laid her mouth on top of his, brushing lightly, tempting him to deepen the kiss. With a sound of raw hunger, he fused their mouths together. The contact immediately made them insane, frantic. Tongues met, flicked against each other, then tangled ferociously. She buried her fingers in his hair, used her grip to pull him closer. He pushed his thick erection against her belly, proving he was ready to give and receive pleasure. Rough hands fell to her ass, smoothed over the round cheeks, and squeezed. A growl erupted from his throat, mingling with her surprised whimper. Ruby felt the material being drawn upward, toward her waist, baring her bottom for his kneading hands.

"Christ, baby, I need to—"

"Do it." She cried out as the sting of his palm against her naked flesh reverberated through her entire body, creating a heaviness between her thighs. "Troy, I need you. Now."

He tore his mouth away from her neck. "I can't take being away from you much longer. If bringing you home means giving you space, I'll do it." His mouth moved over hers in a hot, provocative kiss. "I'd kill to fuck you right now, but not if it sets us back."

Ruby grasped his face in her hands, locked her gaze with his. His pupils were dilated, cheekbones flushed red. "The only way you'll make it worse is if you don't take me back into the stockroom. Let's take what we both need." She traced his bottom lip with her tongue. "Don't you want to feel how wet I am?"

A harsh noise escaped him. "I don't need to touch your pussy to know it's dripping for me. But fuck, I want to. I want to lick it clean."

"I need that, too," she moaned at his ear.

"You need *me*."

"Yes."

Before the word fully escaped her mouth, he wrapped his

hand around her wrist and they were walking at a fast clip back toward the stockroom. He slammed the door and locked it behind them. Immediately, he unbuttoned his shirt and shed it, all the while watching her with erotic intention, as if plotting exactly how he would take her. She started to remove her dress, but he stopped her with a barked command.

"Leave it." Troy's white undershirt came off next, revealing his rigid wall of muscle. Broad chest, tapering into narrow hips, a black path of hair disappearing into his pants. The man knew how his body affected her, and his confidence only increased her craving for him.

He still had his badge and handcuffs clipped to his uniform belt, but when he started to remove them after he'd put aside his gun, she stopped him with a breathless whisper. "Leave them."

She watched his eyes darken seconds before he spun her around. "Now I see what you want. A little role-play to justify letting me have you while you're angry?" He pressed his mouth to her ear, his voice raw. "You won't make this impersonal. I won't let you."

"Do what you have to do." She punctuated her challenge by turning her head and nipping his lip with her teeth.

"I'm too far gone not to oblige you."

"Good. No holding back."

He stepped back. "Reach under your dress and remove your panties," he growled. "Lower them all the way to the floor. Don't bend your legs or you'll get the best use of my hand."

His authoritative tone sent her senses reeling. It was perfect, exactly what she needed. To break away from herself for a brief while. "Yes, Officer." Ruby slipped her thumbs beneath the lacy sides of her thong and glided them slowly down her hips and thighs. She knew at what point her bare bottom showed because she heard him curse, followed by the sound of his belt unbuckling.

"Go sit on the edge of the desk," he rasped. "Open your legs."

She did as instructed, but couldn't help sliding her hands up her rib cage to cup her breasts. Their tips were puckered, begging for contact. The smooth, cool desk felt illicit against her flesh without the benefit of clothing to serve as a barrier. When Troy moved between her thighs, her eyes slipped shut and she tipped her face up, desperate for his mouth. Instead, her hands were pulled behind her back and bound together with a click of the cuffs. Ruby's breath escaped in an excited rush.

"You want your breasts played with?" He drew her neckline low and slipped a hand inside to cup her. "It's going to cost you some of the time I'd have spent between your legs, worshiping your delicious little clit." He licked his upper lip, the movement causing her belly to tighten. "Which is it? I've got an aching hard-on for you and I'm impatient to fuck."

She whimpered. "Both. I want both."

Having her hands restrained behind her back naturally caused her back to arch, but when Troy yanked her top down, Ruby couldn't help but bow her spine further and present her breasts, offering them up to his mouth. When his tongue dragged over her right nipple, red-hot lust shot straight to her core. He sampled her other breast in the same manner, slowly, teasingly, until she begged incoherently for more. Finally, he drew a nipple into his mouth and sucked long and hard. The pull in her belly felt like an assault on her sanity. Legs spread wide on the desk, her bottom circled, tempting him closer, but he wouldn't come. With her hands cuffed, she couldn't use her hands to pull his hips against hers.

"Yes, baby." A long pull on her nipple. "I know what you want. You want to wiggle your wet pussy all over my lap and turn me into a madman. Too bad. The next thing you feel between your legs will be my tongue."

"Please…just do it *now*."

He flicked his tongue out, curling it around one stiff peak. "What happens to impatient girls who try to tell their man what to do in bed?"

She stifled a sob of pleasure. "They have to wait longer."

"Correct." He dropped to his knees in front of the desk. Lips grazing the insides of her thighs, Troy draped her legs over his shoulders. Panting with anticipation, Ruby moaned when he bit the inside of her knee gently, trailed higher with his wet mouth, then bit her again. He transferred his attention back and forth between the soft skin of her inner thighs, placing bites, until his mouth reached her center. She bit her lip hard to refrain from begging and was rewarded with a stiff-tongued lick directly over her clitoris.

"Troy!" Her body shuddered violently. "Please, more. Please."

His answering growl vibrated through her system. "Christ. How long has it been since I've gone down on you? Three days? Four? That's a fucking sin." He scooped his hands beneath her bottom and hauled her hips toward his mouth. "Let me get a fix, baby."

The suction of his mouth robbed her of rational thought. With a strangled moan, she fell back on her restrained hands, legs falling open as if boneless. His skilled mouth moved over her as if for the first time. He couldn't get close enough, even lifting her bottom clear off the table to get a better angle to perform his blissful torture. Every time she felt the orgasm tightening her belly, tingling in her limbs, he took her higher. Held her back. And each time her release loomed brighter, more intense, until finally he had mercy on her. The tip of his tongue placed firm pressure over her clitoris, rubbing back and forth rapidly, easing and strengthening until her world caved in around her. In the distance, she heard herself yelling, but the exquisite squeezing of her sex overpowered everything else.

Troy slammed into her while she was still midorgasm, sending her senses reeling. The sudden fullness inside her clenching center pushed her over the edge again immediately. Her hips were lifted off the desk, supported by Troy's strong forearm as he brought her down hard on his erection, over and over. When their mouths fused together in a kiss, the blistering contact cut off screams she hadn't even been aware of issuing. The only sound left was wet, slapping flesh and Troy's loud grunts of pleasure.

He tore away with a curse and worked his hips faster. "Hot, slippery girl." Her ass hit the desk, giving Troy more leverage. At an angle, he drove deep, giving her a swift, accurate pounding. "Did you need Officer Bennett to come by and give you a nice hard ride?" Without pausing in his assault, he wrenched her thighs wider. "Well? How the fuck am I doing?"

Ruby shuddered as his words tempted another release. "Fucking amazing. Perfect. Don't stop, don't stop, *don't stop.*"

"Go on, baby. Tighten up and come again." He pressed their foreheads together, locking his gaze with hers. "As soon as you do, I'm going to sink all the way in, to the back of your pussy. I'm going to do what only I have the privilege of doing. And you're going to take my seed and love it."

Ruby's eyes went blind; her head fell back. Dizzying heat and relief raced through her veins as Troy followed through on his promise. His hoarse cries against her neck only prolonged the moment as she came down from the highest peak she'd ever known.

Suddenly, the feelings were too much to bear. Her emotions felt battered. She was drowning in them and needed something to hold on to, to ground herself, but her hands were cuffed behind her back. Uselessly, she pulled at the restraints, metal clanking loudly on the desk. A loud, frustrated sob racked her chest.

Troy pulled back, horror dawning on his face. "Ruby. Baby, what's wrong…did I—"

"Uncuff me," she croaked.

Quickly, he drew the keys from his pants pocket. When her wrists slipped free, she sucked in a relieved breath, but it released on a shaky cry. The events of the last week blasted her like a tidal wave. Her father returning, fighting with Troy, dealing with deeply buried emotions concerning her mother. She'd been keeping it firmly tucked beneath the surface, but the dam had finally burst. Tears she couldn't control poured down her cheeks.

Troy moved in front of her, taking her face in his hands. He looked tortured, ripped apart by her unexplained grief. "Talk to me. I'm dying here." She looked up into the eyes of the man she loved beyond reason and knew, beyond a shadow of a doubt, that *he* was her anchor. No matter what happened, no matter how they fought, he would be there, standing firmly in her corner. Without giving herself a chance to second-guess, she threw her arms around Troy and pulled him close. With an unsteady exhale, he held her tight against his chest, rocking her back and forth.

"I love you," she whispered. "No matter what happens."

"Nothing is going to happen to you," he responded fiercely.

She swallowed hard. "The match is tomorrow night."

Troy stiffened slightly, telling her he hadn't known. Her father must have sensed the temporary weakness in their bond the other night and cut him out of the loop. "Are you going to let me come with you or do I have to—"

"Go behind my back?" Troy didn't respond and Ruby sighed. "Come with me. You'll show up either way."

"Damn right."

She pulled back to meet his eyes. "Whatever is going on between us...I won't let you get hurt. Not because of me. Remember that."

He looked like he wanted to argue, but wisely didn't address her cryptic remark. "Tomorrow night. I'll pick you up. We walk in together."

She nodded, wondering if they would walk out the same way.

Chapter Seven

Troy positioned himself between Ruby and the group of four men scrutinizing them from across the dim pool hall. His first instinct upon seeing where the match would take place had been to break the speed limit driving her back to Manhattan. Located in a section of Jersey City that hadn't yet seen the same revitalization as neighboring areas, Mancuso's didn't even have a proper sign or entrance. Around the back of an out-of-business furniture store, MANCUSO'S was painted sloppily over a dented metal door that let out into an alleyway, where Troy had parked his car. *Pool hall* was honestly a loose description for what was in reality a basement directly beneath the old furniture store. None of the pool tables matched, and the wooden bar looked so distinctly out of place, Troy had a hunch it had been "borrowed" from somewhere else.

He checked his phone again, in an attempt to distract himself from the fact that Ruby looked completely unfazed by their shady surroundings, reminding him she'd been in this situation too many times to count. Upon entering, she'd tossed the men, one of them an uncle she'd never met, a disinterested glance before screwing her pool stick together, leaning against the wall and promptly looking as bored as possible. Part of him fucking loved her for that. Yet knowing it was an act, the rest of him just wanted to throw her over his shoulder and carry her out of there, damn the consequences.

Seeing that his friends still hadn't called him with any news, Troy bit back a curse and shoved his phone back into his pocket. Shit. They were running out of time. He reminded himself that Daniel, Brent, and Matt were busting their asses trying to locate Ruby's mother before this game began, but as time wore on, that possibility seemed less and less likely. The woman had made it damn near impossible to trace her, but as of this evening, they'd been closing in on her. He'd had to leave the station to pick up Ruby, leaving his three friends to put the final pieces together. Thankfully, he didn't think he could find three more dedicated or capable cops to pick up the slack in his absence.

Troy hoped Jim never showed up. Or at least gave them a little more time to retrieve the information that would render this dangerous game unnecessary. He started to check his phone for the umpteenth time since they'd entered the hall, but the metal door creaked open and slammed, bringing his head up.

His body tensed and he took a step closer to Ruby, but instead of Jim walking through the entrance, Bowen swaggered in. He took in the entire place in one sweeping glance, through an eye Troy had blackened less than forty-eight hours ago.

"He always has to make a damn entrance," Ruby muttered.

Obviously loving everyone's focus on him, Bowen shivered dramatically. "It's colder than a mother-in-law's heart in here." He didn't wait for a reply, but strode toward their side of the hall and sat a short distance away from him and Ruby. Troy glanced back at her and she gave a small shake of her head, telling him she hadn't asked Bowen to come. Noticing the tension that had crept into Ruby's shoulders the second Bowen walked in, Troy made a decision. She already had enough pressure on her without their antagonism adding to it, and he wouldn't allow the elephant in the room to stand between them a second longer.

Troy cleared his throat and jerked his chin at Bowen, signaling him over. Warily, Bowen stood and complied, arms crossed over his chest. "Yeah?"

"Listen, Driscol. I owe you an apology." Bowen's and Ruby's identical double takes were comical. Or would have been, if the three of them weren't standing in a decrepit basement in New Jersey, waiting to play a uniquely staked pool game against criminals. *The things you do for love.* "Instead of fighting against having you in her life...I should have been thanking you. For looking out for her when I couldn't. All right? So, thank you."

After a moment wherein Troy guessed Bowen was trying to gauge his sincerity, he nodded uncomfortably. "Okay, man. It's no big deal."

Watching Bowen's tough-guy demeanor momentarily lift, Troy felt a stab of guilt. Bowen was just as lost as Ruby had been once, but he didn't have anyone to pull him toward the light. No one except Ruby. And he'd been trying to take that away from him. "No, it is a big deal. I owe you."

"Fine. That's...fine." Bowen yanked at the collar of his jacket. "Jesus. What does a guy have to do to get a drink around here?"

Troy stifled a smile, then glanced at Ruby. His breath caught at the look on her face. Fierce and beautiful emotion shone in her eyes, telling him he'd finally done something right. *About time, Troy. And not a moment too soon.*

"I love you," she mouthed.

He winked at her. *Later*, Troy tried to communicate with his eyes. Later he'd tell her how much he loved her. Then he'd show her continuously, until their bodies gave out. A wave of impatience swept over him. He wanted this over, so he could take Ruby back home where she would be safe. As if his thoughts had conjured Ruby's father, the rusted front door opened and Jim Elliott breezed in.

His attention swung between the group positioned at the bar and Ruby. "Oh, good. I was worried the party would start without me."

One of the men stepped forward into the sparse light, his face a mask of irritation. Ruby's uncle, Robert Bell, Troy guessed, based on his coloring and position within the group. "Not a wise move to keep me waiting, Elliott."

"No? I guess that's a matter of opinion."

The group of men shifted in irritation. "My opinion is the only one that matters here."

Troy could practically feel the surge of energy shoot through Ruby. He knew then, there was a part of his girl that would always thrive on the prospect of danger. That trait was part of her, something she'd been born with, and it was time he fully accepted it. Hell, he should be thankful for it. God knew their physical relationship required a healthy appreciation for danger. Not to mention, his job was infinitely more risky. Yet she'd never asked him to change. Not once.

God, I need to get her out of here. Need to tell her.

"Let's agree to disagree for expediency's sake." Jim smiled at the angry man as he removed his coat. "Shall we knock some balls around?"

• • •

Ruby tried not to scrutinize her long-lost uncle too closely as she lined up a shot on the seven ball. Theirs had not been a tearful, Oprah-style reunion. Oh no. After they'd flipped a coin to determine who would break the first rack, there had been zero interaction between them. In order to win, she needed to best him at least three out of five games. So far, they'd each won two, making this the final game to decide the winner.

Something about her game was decidedly off. She knew it, and based on Bowen's and her father's tense expressions, they knew it, too. Those two lost games should have been hers, no question. Her uncle had a decent technique, but no heart. No instinct. She'd beat better players than him before with very little effort. She couldn't help feeling distracted, though. Her uncle…something about him filled her with a sense of dread, but she couldn't name the cause. Ruby never forgot a face, so she knew they had never met, but he looked so damn familiar. It didn't make any sense.

The seven ball just missed the side pocket and she heard her father hiss behind her. Bowen frowned at the table, looking confused. No wonder. That hadn't been a difficult shot. Struggling to keep the panic from her face, Ruby leaned against the wall and focused on Troy. He smiled at her, no visible worry on his face, his confidence in her unwavering. A lump formed in her throat, regret washing over her. She suddenly wished she'd never agreed to this. *Look at what you've done. Put Troy, Bowen, and yourself in danger, all for a woman who never wanted anything to do with you.*

At that moment, she wanted to be at home, stretched out beside Troy in their bed, so badly her chest ached with the desire. As if sensing her regretful thoughts, Troy nodded calmly, miraculously steadying her enough to draw a deep breath and focus. An odd look crossed Troy's face then as he dug his phone out of his pocket. Ruby didn't have time to speculate on who would be calling or texting him now, because her uncle missed a bank shot to sink the eleven ball, sending her back to the table.

Focus, Ruby. Three shots and you're out. Put the seven in the side like you should have done before. Use a little right-hand English to send the cue ball down to the opposite end of the table, giving you a corner shot on the three. The eight was a tough shot before, up against the rail, but he just did you a favor by knocking it out. You've accomplished run-outs way more complicated than this. Get out of your head now and win this motherfucker.

She leaned over the table, ready to take her shot. One of Robert's men made a loud, disgusting *smooch* noise. It set her teeth on edge, but she ultimately ignored it. She'd dealt with worse in the past. Troy, however, didn't seem capable of letting it pass.

"Ruby." Troy's deep voice behind her caused her to straighten and turn. At once, the already-thick tension in the room tripled. He took a step toward her. "Let's go. We're out of here."

"W-what? I—"

Red-faced, her father jumped off his stool. "Not happening. You can't just interrupt a goddamn match."

"I can do whatever the hell I want. So can Ruby." His voice cracked like a whip. "And she knows she doesn't have to put up with this bullshit. Not anymore."

Bowen moved in between Troy and her father. "Let's take it easy."

"You shut the fuck up, Driscol." Jim pointed a shaking finger at Ruby, who was still trying to get her head around the fact that Bowen was playing peacekeeper for once. "Finish the match."

She turned back to Troy, who gave her a quiet, meaningful look. Something just underneath his irritation begged for her cooperation. "Don't finish the game." *Trust me,* his eyes added.

Trust had nothing to do with it. Stopping a match before

its completion was tantamount to treason among this group. Putting down her stick and walking away would be a bold move. Troy, being intelligent and well-acquainted with her world by now, knew it. So he had to have a very good reason for telling her to stop. She had to believe in him. Slowly, Ruby lowered the butt of her cue to the floor.

Robert spoke up. "This is a business transaction. No one leaves until it's over."

In her peripheral vision, Ruby saw a few of her uncle's men step forward, toward Troy, whose hand slipped into his jacket. Surprisingly, Bowen moved to stand next to him, both of them clearly ready to fight to get her out of there without finishing the game. Quickly, she ran the numbers in her head. Five against two. Troy had his department-issued gun on him, but she was willing to bet her uncle's men were all armed, too. The thought of gunfire exploding in the room made her blood freeze. No, she couldn't let them get hurt on her behalf. Not when three pool balls were the only thing standing between them and walking out the door unharmed.

"Everyone stop," Ruby demanded. "I'll finish the game."

"Ruby—"

"It'll be over in one minute," she said softly, pleading with her eyes for Troy to understand. "Then we'll go home."

Her uncle snorted. "You're that confident?"

"I'm always confident." She jerked her chin toward the table. "You screwed yourself by knocking the eight ball off the rail. It was the only shot that had me worried. Watch and learn, *uncle*."

She ignored her dad's proud laugh, putting her sole focus on winning the game and getting them safely out the door. At this point, the information about her mother came secondary. She took a deep breath and chalked her cue, then bent low to put the seven ball into the side pocket. Next came the three. She quickly rounded the table, gesturing with her stick toward the pocket where she intended to sink the eight. Her uncle acknowledged her calling of the pocket with a low grunt. Ruby tried to suppress the hum in her veins, the distinct feeling that came with being in the zone. It had been missing the entire match, but now she felt it, giving her tunnel vision and blurring everything out but the table. Without giving herself a chance to become distracted, Ruby lined up her shot and sank the eight ball.

Before she'd fully straightened from the table, Ruby felt Troy move in behind her, one hand coming to rest on her hip. Under the pretense of kissing her neck, he whispered in her ear. "No matter what happens, stay calm."

Maintaining her practiced poker face, she nodded absently and began to unscrew her stick.

"She beat you fair and square, Robert." Jim cocked a hip against the pool table. "Give me what I came for."

Ruby narrowed her gaze. "Don't you mean, what *we* came for?"

A shadow crossed Jim's face as he shrugged. "Sure."

She'd known it all along, that her father had an ulterior motive, but having it confirmed felt like a slap in the face. Quickly, she ducked her head to hide the embarrassing tears that sprang to her eyes, grateful for Troy's comforting presence at her back.

Robert hadn't yet responded to Jim, so he prompted him again. "So, tell me. Where can I find my infamous ex-girlfriend, Pamela Bell?"

A manila file folder slapped down in the center of the pool table, presumably with her mother's whereabouts inside. Ruby's eyes shot wide when some of the documents spilled out, including an old, grainy photograph. Jim snatched up the papers immediately, but not before she'd seen the smiling picture of her mother staring back at her. Denial hit her quickly. What she'd seen had to have been a mistake. But on the heels of her denial came the resounding reminder that nothing, *nothing* is a coincidence.

Mya Hicks. Her coworker, investor, friend…was her mother?

Momentarily, her deafening heartbeat drowned out the loud conversation taking place around her, but Troy's steady hand squeezing her hip brought her back to earth. Needing him to steady her, Ruby leaned back against his hard chest for balance. Sliding a possessive arm around her midsection, he gave her some much-needed support. *No matter what happens, stay calm*, he'd said. Ruby took a deep breath and slid her cue into its leather carrying case.

"So, Jim. Are you going to share my mother's information with me or am I wasting my breath?"

Across the table, Robert laughed incredulously, apparently recovered from his loss. "Is that what he told you? That he'd share?" He shook his head. "No, Jim has a score to settle with my crazy-ass sister. If you think he'll let anything get in the way of that, you don't know your father very well."

Upon hearing Mya was in trouble, Ruby struggled to keep her features schooled. They needed to get out of there and warn her right away. She could sort through her feelings and figure out the rest later. First step? *Don't be obvious.* "No, I'd say I know him better than anyone," she said quietly, slinging her pool cue over her shoulder. "What did she do to you?"

Jim tapped the file against his thigh, considering her through an unreadable mask. "Besides sleeping with my best friend at the time and taking off with one hundred thousand dollars of my hard-earned money?" He shrugged his broad shoulders. "Without going into details, she saw something she wasn't meant to see. You can use your imagination. Being the agreeable man that I am, I told her to get out of town and never show her face here again or we'd have a problem. Funny, I never mentioned cleaning out my bank account as a bon voyage gift."

Ruby absorbed that as calmly as possible, but her mind caught on one confusing detail. She frowned. "But, your best friend—"

"Let's get her out of here," Bowen said abruptly, coming up beside her and Troy.

Troy took her hand. "My thoughts exactly."

Chapter Eight

Keeping Ruby sandwiched between them, Troy and Bowen led her from Mancuso's. Troy kept a steady eye on Robert's group of friends as they passed, baring his teeth when one of them looked at Ruby's ass and groaned theatrically. The entire time she'd been playing the match, hell, since the moment they'd arrived, he'd wanted nothing more than to wipe the lecherous expressions from their faces. The telltale bulge of their concealed weapons had forced him to keep a level head, not easy where Ruby and ogling men were concerned, but the thought of her anywhere near gunfire had forced him to remain calm.

Until he'd received the text message from Daniel, and he'd been forced to use their obscene behavior as a way to get Ruby out of the bar. Not that it had worked.

As soon as they cleared the exit, putting the three of them alone in the alley, Ruby tried to pull away from him, obviously intending to run for his car. "We have to hurry. She's…it's Mya. I know where she is. I know—"

Troy grabbed her wrist and stopped her. "So do I. She's at

our apartment."

"*What?*" She and Bowen asked simultaneously.

He divided a glance between them. "As always, your faith in my police work is humbling." Hesitant relief transformed Ruby's worried look, tension ebbing from her body as he spoke. "We've been working on locating her for days. Right before you took those last three shots, Daniel texted me that they'd found her. He explained everything to her and she's been taken to our place. She's out of Jim's reach. For now. We'll need to—"

Ruby threw herself into his arms. "Thank you," she whispered into his ear.

He squeezed her tight. "There's nothing I wouldn't do for you, Ruby. You know that."

"I know. I love you." Her quick exhale fanned his neck. "I can't believe Mya is my mother."

Inhaling her scent greedily, Troy nodded. "Baby, I really need to get you out of this dark alley in New Jersey before I have heart failure."

A shaky laugh escaped her. "Okay, let's go." Reluctantly, they parted, both searching the darkness in confusion.

"Where's Bowen?" Troy asked, realizing they were alone in the alley, Bowen nowhere to be seen.

After a beat, Ruby sighed and started for the car. "He'll show up again when he's ready."

Forty-five minutes later, they stood outside their apartment door. On the other side, he could hear pacing, layered above the television. On the way in, he'd double-checked to make sure Brent was stationed outside in his squad car, as promised. Knowing Jim might already be on his way to Mya's apartment, ready to break and enter if necessary, Troy had asked Daniel to remove any trace of Mya's professional ties to Ruby from the woman's apartment. But Jim Elliott was a smart man. He would make the connection sooner or later.

Mya wouldn't be able to remain in their apartment forever. Until tonight, he hadn't been aware that Ruby's mother was a potential witness against Jim, making her proximity to Ruby all the more dangerous. The longer she stayed, the more risk mounted for Ruby. Troy would prevent that at all costs.

Before turning the key in the lock, Troy paused. "Are you ready?"

"Yeah." Ruby shook her head as if to clear it. "This is stupid. I spend every day with her. It's just Mya in there."

He brushed his thumb over her jaw. "Because it's different now."

"Yeah." She blew out a breath. "I never let myself think too hard about my mother, but now I have a thousand questions. I don't even know where to start."

Troy started to answer, but the door swung open, revealing Mya. Silhouetted by light, her face was obscured by shadows, but her relief at seeing Ruby unharmed was unmistakable. She steadied herself with a hand on the doorjamb as lessening tension deflated her. "Don't you know never to go to New Jersey on days ending in Y?"

Ruby crossed her arms, chin going up a notch. "What, are you my mother or something?"

A beat of silence passed, before both of their mouths edged up into hesitant smiles. Mya stepped back to let them into the apartment. "I deserve that."

"You think?"

Mya rubbed her arms vigorously and nodded toward the living room. "Can we talk? Alone?"

Wanting to give them their privacy to hash things out, Troy nodded encouragingly at Ruby and headed for the bedroom, but she snagged his hand before he'd made it two steps. "I want to talk. But Troy stays. We don't have any secrets." She looked at him meaningfully. "Never again."

Christ, if they didn't have an audience at that moment,

he would have kissed her within an inch of her life. He let the feeling of happiness replace the dread he'd been experiencing for days, allowing himself to simply be grateful for her. For what they had.

Just for a moment, Troy wanted to stop mentally replaying the ways he'd almost lost her, everything he had to do to keep her, and what his life would be like without her. Instead, he pulled her onto his lap on the couch and enjoyed her familiar weight. Her hand, so trusting, in his. His girl needed his support and he was all too ready to provide it, for as long as she'd have him.

• • •

Ruby stared at Mya and tried to reconcile her former wild-child employee with the woman she'd subconsciously created to fill in the gaps since childhood. It made sense now. The immediate bond she'd felt for Mya from day one. She'd always wondered about it, but had ultimately decided to count herself lucky instead of thinking too deeply about it. That female bond had been lacking in her life, and the sudden appearance of it had made her uncomfortable enough to push it aside. Not inspect it for flaws or inconsistencies.

Now that she knew what to look for, their relationship became glaringly obvious. Ruby didn't know if she was projecting the resemblance she suddenly craved like air, but she saw it nonetheless. Underneath her piercings and heavy eyeliner, her mother looked back at her.

"Are you just going to stare at me all night?"

Yup. Definitely my mother. Based on Troy's grunt behind her, he'd had the same thought. She elbowed him gently in the ribs, but he only tightened his hold.

Ruby sat a little straighter on Troy's lap, taking a moment to acknowledge the rightness of having him there for this life-changing conversation. "So, I guess you didn't just have an insatiable interest in the custom pool cue business?"

Mya's lips twitched. "It's growing on me."

"My professor, when he said he had a friend who was interested in investing…?"

"We were sleeping together."

Ruby wrinkled her nose. "All right. We're going to have to set a whole new level of boundaries now that I know you're my mother."

"Boundaries are boring." When Ruby prompted her to continue with silence, Mya sighed. "I asked around the old neighborhood and found out where you were going to school. I might have…met your professor on purpose. Dug around a little bit." She lifted one shoulder and let it drop. "I saw the opportunity to get to know you without any of the inevitable pressure of a reunion. And I took it."

Ruby wasn't fooled by her mother's seeming nonchalance. She recognized the blasé attitude Mya was using to camouflage her true feelings. Underneath all of it lay vulnerability. A fear of rejection. If she hadn't been concerned about Ruby's reaction to her sudden reappearance, she would have simply approached her, without any of the false pretense. As if reading her thoughts, Mya looked away.

"Why now?"

Mya looked up at the ceiling as if searching for an answer. "I left because I wanted to see the world outside of Brooklyn. At some point, it stopped being about discovering myself and more about avoiding. I cut the bullshit and came back." Her throat worked. "I thought about you all the time. Figured I'd come see what you were up to."

"You should have told me who you were. I don't like being played, Mya."

"Pamela." Her mother held up a hand. "And you're right. I'd be angry, too." She glanced around at the apartment. "It's just…look how well you're doing for yourself. Running your own business. Living on the Upper East Side with your hot boyfriend—"

"Seriously."

Pamela lifted an eyebrow. "Just stating the obvious."

"State less of it." Ruby elbowed Troy again when laughter rumbled in his chest.

"Fine," she relented with a small smile. "Anyway, it didn't feel right to disrupt your happy life."

"It's happy now." Ruby swallowed hard, surprised to feel tears gathering in her eyes for the second time that night. "It hasn't always been this way. Far from it."

Finally, Pamela's careful control slipped, a flash of anguish crossing her face. "I know. I'm sorry."

Ruby nodded, suddenly wanting to flee the living room and the entire emotionally draining scene. She appeased herself by changing the subject. Someday they would get into those childhood years she'd spent living in dingy motel rooms or ducking down in the backseat of Jim's car in case of gunfire. Not tonight, though. It was too soon. Something else weighed on her mind just then. "So should I assume the money you invested in my business was stolen from my father?"

Pamela fell back against her chair with a shaky sigh. "Only a portion. Most of it was mine, though. You'd be surprised what you save on rent when you work as a roadie nine months out of the year."

A roadie. Of course she'd been a roadie. "If given the choice, I never would have touched a dime of Jim's money."

Her mother studied her closely. "I still have most of the money. Maybe deep down, I didn't want to touch it, either."

Ruby didn't respond to that. She hadn't had enough time to process what she wanted to do about her business being built, even partially, on a foundation of illegal cash. "Whatever you saw must have been pretty bad if he wants to kill you for simply showing your face back here. What—"

Troy stiffened behind her, and Pamela shook her head adamantly. "It's safer if you don't know."

Her boyfriend's body deflated and once again she felt staggered by his protectiveness. "You know, if it wasn't for Troy, there's a strong possibility Jim might have already gotten to you."

Pamela bit her lip and nodded at Troy. "I realize that. Thank you, Troy."

Troy acknowledged her gratitude with a nod that bumped his chin into Ruby's shoulder. A sudden wave of love for him almost toppled her. She knew he felt it, too, when he squeezed her hand and brought it up to his mouth.

"I also know you did it for my daughter. No other reason."

"It's the only one I'll ever need," he answered steadily.

Pamela laughed to herself. "Good Lord, I wish I'd had your taste in men when it was young enough to matter."

Her mother's comment brought the memory of her father's words back to her then. *Besides sleeping with my best friend at the time and taking off with one hundred thousand dollars of my hard-earned money?* Obviously she'd only gotten half the story, but tomorrow would be soon enough to find out the rest. She'd learned more than enough tonight already, and frankly, she wasn't quite ready to open a discussion about her mother two-timing her father. Right now, she wanted nothing more than to crawl into bed with Troy and let him soothe away her father's betrayal, her mother's lying to her about her identity for months…all of it.

"I know how lucky I am." Ruby stood and pulled Troy to his feet, stifling a shiver when his full height caused him to look down at her from a good six inches above. With difficulty, she looked back at her mother. "Can we talk more in the morning?"

Pamela gave a half smile. "It's not as if I can go anywhere."

Ruby nodded stiffly, not remotely ready to let her mother off the hook by sharing the joke, then led Troy from the room. At the end of the hallway, she pulled him into their bedroom and locked the door. When he looked at her through concerned blue eyes, every thought fled her mind but him. She'd rejected his help this week, pushed him away, yet here he was, standing strong enough for them both. He'd kept the promise he'd made all those months ago. *I'm not going anywhere. I'll never get more than a block away.*

Their nights apart suddenly felt like an unforgivable sin. How had she survived even one night without his arms wrapped around her, his breath even and sure against her neck? His hard body moving over her in the mornings, hot and demanding. Rough hands shoving her legs apart. Mouth growling filthy words against her ear as he pumped his hips faster and faster.

Watching Troy's eyes darken with uncanny awareness so perfectly attuned to her body, Ruby's pulse fluttered wildly, air in her lungs growing short. "We have to be quiet."

"Whatever gets me inside you, hustler."

Her starvation for him shot past the point of unbearable. With a boldness she couldn't suppress, Ruby hooked her hand in his waistband and yanked him toward her. Obviously sensing her need to initiate, Troy simply licked his lips as he watched her unbuckle his belt and unzip his fly, hands flexing at his sides.

"Do I have something hot and wet waiting for me inside those panties, baby?"

She moaned in her throat. "Aren't I always wet and ready for you, Troy?"

His jaw tightened when her hand closed around his rigid erection, teasing him with a light stroke. "You going to talk dirty to me tonight for a change?" His head tipped back when Ruby nodded, exposing his corded throat. "Fuck. You choose the night we have to be quiet to flip the script on me?"

Resolving not to second-guess any of her urges, Ruby shot forward and bit the side of his neck. "You've had trouble keeping quiet ever since I started riding you bareback." She swirled her tongue over the red bite mark. "Will I need to slow down just to keep you from moaning too loud?"

He pulled his shirt over his head, exposing a rock hard muscle that shifted sexily with his every movement. "We both know once you get moving on my cock, there's no slowing down."

Feeling dizzy under the onslaught of anxious need, Ruby pushed him back onto the bed so he sat on the edge. Waiting impatiently to be pleasured, with an air akin to royalty.

A king. *Her* king. He deserved to be treated like one.

Without removing her hot gaze from his, she stripped out of her jeans and panties quickly, then using his wide shoulders for support, she straddled him. When she didn't immediately impale herself on him, Troy growled dangerously, hands gripping the supple flesh of her bottom in warning.

"Ruby, you're sorely underestimating how badly I need to fuck." He took her mouth in an impassioned kiss, forcing her mouth wide and giving her just enough erotic treatment from his tongue to leave her clinging to him. He pulled back to let her suck in air, nipping at her chin and neck.

Ruby struggled back to herself, unwilling to go under his spell so easily this time. She was encountering the fierce desire to reward him for being steadfast, refusing to let their foundation crumble in her moment of weakness. Troy always took control in bed, praising her every movement, sound, reaction. So much of that was the way he spoke to her. Coached her. Could she do that for him? She slid her fingers into his hair and tilted his head to one side, tracing her lips over his ear. "You always need to fuck. It's the kind of man you are. Powerful, insatiable. Dirty."

He traced a path down her chest and sucked her right nipple into his mouth. "You love it dirty, baby girl."

"Damn right," Ruby breathed, reaching behind her to wrap greedy fingers around his thick shaft. With her tongue, she licked along the seam of his lips, at the same time dragging the plump head of his erection through the dampness between her thighs. "I love everything you do to me. Whether you fuck me fast, or slide in and out until I shake, I know you're going to make me come. You do it every time, don't you?"

"Yes," he hissed against her lips, chest shuddering where it pressed to her breasts. "Let me tell you why. Because I'm a fucking addict and satisfying you is how I get high." His hips surged off the bed. "Now stop being such a goddamn cock-tease and put me in."

Ruby didn't need another word of urging. Clamping her teeth down onto her bottom lip to contain the moan, she guided Troy to her entrance and sank down inch by inch. His head fell back when he'd completely filled her, a low growl escaping on a breath. They both took a moment to savor the feeling before Troy began rolling his hips beneath her.

"Move, baby." With one hand, he grasped her bottom hard, possessively. "You know the way I like it."

Ruby brought her feet up, bracing them on either side of his hips on the bed. Using his shoulders for balance, she rose up until just the tip of his erection remained inside of her, then she came down hard with a buck of her hips. She did it again and again, faster each time until she bounced up and down on his lap. Her stomach muscles bunched and released, the flesh between her legs starting to quiver. The look of raw heat on his face only heightened every sensation until she felt seconds from imploding. Wanting to prolong the experience, she slowed her rhythm, dragging her damp mouth over Troy's. "You like that?"

"You know I love it." He fisted her hair in his hand,

dragging her forward for a wet kiss. "And if you stop to ask me another question, I won't give a fuck who's in the next room. Your ass is going to feel both sides of my hand." Whatever he saw on her face made his eyelids droop. "You get off on just talking about it, don't you? Tell me how much you love it, baby."

Losing herself in the moment, her hips began to pump mindlessly. "I love when you spank me. When it hurts..."

"You come harder?" He covered her mouth with his hand, capturing her moan when he tilted his hips, the new angle firing her toward the precipice. "You don't think I know that?"

"Troy. Oh, *God*."

Both hands on her bottom, he began lifting her up and down at a delicious pace. Every time she slid down onto his thick flesh, her orgasm loomed closer. Troy pressed their foreheads together, forcing her to open her eyes and look at him. "Tell me I rule your world, Ruby."

"You rule my world. You know you do."

"Tell me you love me."

"I love you. I *love* you," Ruby chanted, unable to hold back the rush of sensation any longer. Legs clamping hard around his waist, she rode her climax out relentlessly, hips pumping in a blur as Troy came apart beneath her. He shot forward to capture her whimpers with his mouth, swallowing them with throaty groans. Ruby could sense how badly he wanted to raise his hand and slap her bottom, and his hard-won restraint somehow made her orgasm all the more powerful.

When she'd finished shaking, Ruby slumped down into his welcoming embrace and buried her face against his neck. He kissed her hair once, twice, whispering praise and love, words that made her heart swell huge in her chest. Finally, Troy laid them back onto the mattress, still wrapped around each other.

Blue eyes pleaded with hers. "Please don't spend the night away from me anymore."

She traced a pattern on his sweat-slicked chest. "I won't. I promise."

His long release of breath fluttered her hair. "Sleep now. We'll worry about everything in the morning."

Ruby nodded through a yawn. Tomorrow would be soon enough to worry about her father coming after her mother. Tomorrow.

Right before she drifted off, a little voice in the back of her head warned her tomorrow would be too late.

Chapter Nine

Troy locked the door of his police vehicle and headed toward the station at a fast clip. He'd woken early and headed to Brooklyn with the intention of tracking down Jim, but he'd had no luck. In truth, he hadn't really expected Ruby's father to show himself in his old neighborhood. Surprisingly, he hadn't shown up at Pamela's apartment last night as they'd expected. Daniel had been waiting with backup to arrest him for breaking and entering, a short-term solution to keep him off the street until they could figure out where to put Pamela. Now Troy began to worry that Jim had either spotted the police lying in wait, or they'd somehow tipped their hand yesterday at Mancuso's.

Whatever it was, he didn't like it. Something didn't feel right. Until today, he'd been able to predict Jim's moves accurately, but since this morning, he'd started feeling as though he'd underestimated the man. The entire drive back from Brooklyn, he'd been racking his brain for something he'd failed to see. Last night in Mancuso's, Jim's eagerness to confront Pamela had been palpable. There had to be a reason he'd neglected to go straight to her apartment.

He had a sudden vision of how beautiful Ruby had looked, curled up beside him in their bed this morning, bathed in predawn light. Her hair had been a tangled mess on the pillow, courtesy of him waking her in the middle of the night for a quick, pounding fuck. Christ, as soon as he'd stretched out on top of her, she'd been frantic for him, as if they hadn't made love just hours before. He'd been forced to hold her down and cover her mouth to keep her quiet. And damn, he'd loved every frantic, sweaty second of it.

She was counting on him. The giving of trust last night had been a tangible thing and it weighed heavily on his shoulders. He couldn't let her down.

Troy came to a dead stop when he heard the gun cocking behind him. He didn't even have to turn around to know who held it.

"Holding a gun on me outside the police station?" Troy turned slowly, hand itching to reach for his own weapon. "You're either desperate or stupid."

Jim shrugged. "Either of those options makes you dead if you touch your gun."

Troy whistled under his breath. "You know, this whole meet-your-girlfriend's-father thing is really turning out to be a pain in the ass."

"You know, under different circumstances, I might have liked you." He pointed the gun at Troy's midsection. "But probably not. Put your gun, cell phone, and whatever other police bullshit you're holding on the ground and slide them over to me."

"Go fuck yourself." As confident as he sounded, Troy knew he was at a disadvantage. This early in the morning, only a handful of cops were inside the station and most of them were exhausted from the night shift. There were cameras all over the parking lot, but only an off chance someone was inside monitoring them. That footage was only accessed if an incident took place, but it would happen after the fact. His only chance was to stall and hope another cop arrived to distract Jim long enough for him to draw his weapon. On top of everything, the possibility of having to injure or kill Ruby's father made him ill.

Jim laughed without humor. "You've got balls, I'll give you that. I guess I shouldn't be surprised. Can't imagine my daughter dating a pushover."

"Damn right."

His tone turned almost conversational, but amusement lurked in his eyes. "You must hate me like hell, knowing the situations I put her in. Did she ever tell you about the time we lost that match in Duluth, Minnesota? I left her as collateral until I could pawn my gold ring to pay up." When Troy's hands curled into fists, Jim laughed. "Relax, it was only for about an hour."

"I was conflicted about killing you before. Not any longer."

"You won't get the chance."

Troy's jaw tightened painfully. "What the hell do you want?"

"I'll have what I want soon enough." Jim raised the gun slightly higher. "For now, though? I have to tie up some loose ends. Namely you." He jerked his chin toward a blue Impala idling at the curb about sixty yards away, just outside police station property. "You're coming with me."

An incredulous laugh escaped him. "Keep dreaming."

"I had a feeling you'd say that. It's why I stopped by your apartment this morning to pay my daughter and her bitch mother a visit. They put up quite a fight." His smile widened maliciously. "If you come with me, I might be willing to let Ruby off with a warning. You, on the other hand, don't get one."

Troy's blood turned to ice. His heart lodged in his throat, choking off his air, but he tried desperately not to let his sickening fear show. *No, no, no.* "Her mother? You're losing your touch, Jim. Ruby hasn't seen her since she was a child."

"You must think I'm an idiot."

Troy simply raised an eyebrow in response, even though he wanted to wrap his hands around the older man's throat.

Jim shifted impatiently, obviously having expected them to be gone by now. "Look, I knew I was racing the clock this week. You're a goddamn cop. I knew you would try to find Ruby's mother before me. But when you let her walk into Mancuso's last night, it told me you hadn't found her yet. Then you got that phone call and everything changed." He scoffed. "I'm not a blind man. You'd throw yourself in front of a train for my girl, yet you don't even try to take the file away from me? Just walk out whistling Dixie without her getting what she came for? No, I knew then that you'd found her."

Dammit, he'd assumed Jim's greed would blind him to anything but getting what he wanted. It had been a vast underestimation on his part, and it was too late now to do anything about it. Jesus, he could have Ruby tied up somewhere and there was no way he could pick up his cell phone and call Brent to go check, either. Knowing he couldn't go solely on the word of a criminal, Troy shook his head. "You don't have them. It's a bluff. You never would have gotten past the men outside."

"You willing to bet on that? My profession has taught me the importance of being invisible."

Troy understood the meaning of Jim's earlier cryptic statement. If he went with Jim now, he might allow Ruby to go free. Troy wouldn't walk away alive, but at least Ruby would have a chance. He couldn't gamble on the hope that Jim was merely bluffing. If he refused to leave, the possibility existed that Jim might take him out here and now, unwilling to ignore the possibility that Pamela had confided Jim's past crime while at their apartment. If he went willingly, allowing Jim to tie up his loose end, at least he might be able to exchange himself to save Ruby.

There was no choice.

"If you hurt her—"

"Relax, she's just a little bruised up."

Helplessness raged through Troy, the need to get to Ruby almost bringing him to his knees. Reluctantly, he removed his gun and kicked it across the pavement. "Take me to her."

• • •

Ruby frowned down at her cell phone as she waited for coffee to brew.

Pamela walked into the kitchen behind her, still wearing the same ripped jeans and white tank top from the night before. "Is that your pre-coffee face or is something wrong?"

Not quite ready to face her mother yet, Ruby busied herself by pulling two mugs out of the cabinet. Anyway, she didn't know if she could put the anxious feeling into words. It sat in her belly like a metal dumbbell. "It's nothing."

After a pause, Pamela sighed. "Come on. I'm the same person you've been shooting the shit with for months at the workshop. Can we just go to that place for a while until we're ready for the dark and twisty?"

Ruby smiled despite herself, but it quickly vanished. Once again, her eyes strayed to her cell phone. "Every day since we've been together, Troy has texted me when he sits down at his desk. It's like…our thing. He never forgets." She didn't explain Troy's reason for creating the ritual, as yet another way to remind her on a daily basis that he wasn't going anywhere. She'd come to expect the text messages, whether they were sweet or sexual. *Miss you already* or *I'm going to lick what's mine later.* They'd become a constant, like Troy. He hadn't even neglected to send them while they were in the midst of their fight, so Troy forgetting the morning after an incredible night together...it seemed odd, to say the least.

"He's probably just busy doing cop stuff," Pamela said, but Ruby heard a note of uncertainty in her voice, telling her she didn't believe in coincidences, either. As long as Jim remained in town, every anomaly would somehow connect back to him.

"I'm going to give him five more minutes, then I'll call," Ruby decided, pouring them each a mug of coffee. "In the meantime, maybe I'll just give my friend Bowen a call. See if he heard of Jim being anywhere in the old neighborhood last night or this morning."

Pamela's coffee mug paused halfway to her mouth. "Bowen?"

"Yeah. Bowen Driscol." Ruby watched her mother closely, curious over her reaction. She'd purposely never spoken about Bowen before in the workshop, wanting to keep her past separate from her professional life. While she would always count Bowen as her best friend, there was no denying his criminal history. Or *present*, for that matter. It hadn't seemed like a wise move divulging too much to the woman investing so much in her upstart company.

As if she'd pushed her father's unwanted words straight to her subconscious overnight, they suddenly came creeping back in, waving a red flag. He'd claimed Pamela had slept with his best friend *at the time*...but before her mother had taken off, his best friend had been...

Slowly, Ruby lowered herself into a chair. "You cheated with Lenny? Bowen's...father?"

At first, her mother looked startled, but resignation followed on its heels. "I wasn't always the paragon of virtue you see before you today."

"Please, I'm not in the mood for jokes."

Pamela dropped into the chair across from Ruby. "Lenny and I had a...*thing*...long before I hooked up with Jim. I was young and it was exciting, watching them fight over me. Up until that point in my life, no one had given two shits about me."

Ruby sipped her coffee. "I get that."

Regret washed over Pamela's features. "So you do."

Letting the new information sink in about a time before she'd even been born, Ruby frowned. "Wasn't Lenny married back then?"

"No, she was long gone. Took off maybe three years earlier."

Ruby swallowed, trying to ignore the buzzing in her ears. "But...she had to have given birth to Bowen, right? He's four years older than me. If she was long gone..."

Pamela wouldn't look at her, keeping her gaze firmly glued to a spot beyond Ruby's shoulder. It told her everything she needed to know. "Bowen's my—"

"Brother," Pamela interrupted quietly. "Half, anyway."

Everything came back to her in a blinding rush. Bowen's constant, fierce need to protect her from the beginning. Her father's unexplainable hostility toward him. And, worse, the way Bowen had backed down in the face of it, when he'd never backed down from anything in his life.

"H-how long has Bowen known?"

Her mother looked suspiciously close to tears. "Since you were kids. Forever. I started seeing your father shortly after I had Bowen. For a while, I was living with your father, raising you both. Then one day, Lenny came and took him. I couldn't stop him, and your father knew better than to cross Lenny." She rose and walked to the kitchen window. "When he was old enough to understand, Lenny told Bowen to keep his mouth shut. He didn't want any reminder of me in his house. I...I think he may have even threatened your safety if he talked."

When moisture plopped onto Ruby's arm, she realized she'd started crying. All these years, he'd looked out for her, feeling a sense of duty he'd never been allowed to speak about. Just as quickly, her sadness turned to anger. Anger toward the adults who'd played with their children's lives without a thought for anyone but themselves or who it would affect.

She opened her mouth to vocalize the sentiment when her cell phone rang. Relief eclipsed the anger momentarily, as she stood on shaky legs to reach her phone. But it wasn't Troy's number on the screen. A blocked number showed instead.

Her body felt numb as she answered. "Hello?"

"Ruby! Enjoying your reunion with your mother?"

She grabbed on to the counter, her legs unable to support her. No, Jim couldn't have found out so quickly. He was just trying to rattle her. *Please, let that be it.* "What are you talking about?"

Her father's laughter echoed through the phone. "See, this is why I used to do all the talking and you kept your mouth shut and played pool."

"Too bad you usually talked us into more trouble."

Ruby could practically see his cocky shrug through the phone. "More trouble can sometimes equal more money."

God, in that moment, she hated him. How stupid she'd been, allowing herself to hope he cared or felt an ounce of remorse for those years on the road. "Well, at least you have your priorities in order. This conversation is no longer one of mine."

"Hang up and I won't let you say good-bye to your boyfriend." This time, she didn't even try to grab the counter for support as her legs folded beneath her. The pain of her knees landing hard on the linoleum floor barely registered. "Do I have your attention now?"

"I don't believe you," she whispered, her entire being screaming in denial. Still, another part of her, which knew her father better than anyone, heard the rare note of truth in his voice. She also knew what it meant and could hardly breathe through the debilitating dread.

"Would you like to talk to him?"

Ruby deflated under the weight of the confirmation that he had Troy. "Yes," she managed.

In the background, she heard movement and a few muffled words being exchanged before Troy's voice reached her though the phone. "Ruby, stay where you are and call the police," he ordered in a rush. "Do *not* come here."

"Come *where*?" she wailed as a sickening thud, followed by a grunt, assaulted her ear. "Where are you?"

A moment later, her father came back on the line, sounding supremely irritated. "I'd seriously advise you not to listen to him."

"Don't hurt him, please. *Please*." Ruby commanded herself to sit up and focus, even though she wanted to curl up on the floor and never move again. "What do you want? Just tell me."

"I'm going to text you an address. Bring your thief mother to me and I'll let you leave with your boyfriend."

Ruby shook her head rapidly, forgetting in her fear that he couldn't see her. It would never happen. He'd never let them both walk.

"It shouldn't even be a choice, really. What did your mother ever do for you? It's your boyfriend or your mother, Ruby. Make the right choice. We'll be here waiting. You've got an hour." She thought he'd hung up, but he delivered one final parting shot before the line went dead. "And if you call the cops, or alert the one sitting outside guarding your building, Troy will be dead long before they take me."

Her entire body shook as the phone dropped from her

lifeless fingers onto the counter. Only then did she remember her mother was standing beside her.

"He wants me," Pamela guessed. "He wants the money back."

Ruby nodded dumbly. "I won't do it. How can he ask me to—" She flinched when the text message signal went off on her phone. With the address etched permanently on her brain, Ruby turned and tripped her way to the bedroom, shedding her robe and sleep T-shirt as she went. She didn't think, *couldn't* think, as she dragged on a pair of jeans and yanked a hoodie over her head. Until she saw Troy's Chicago Cubs ball cap perched on their dresser, she managed to hold it together, but now she couldn't help the scream that ripped from her throat.

Your fault. This is all your fault. If she'd listened to Troy and refused her father's offer the first night in Quincy's, his life wouldn't be in danger. She'd done this to him. To them.

She had to fix her mistake at all costs.

Ruby shoved her feet into an old pair of Converse and sprinted from the bedroom. "All right, here's what we're going to do." An empty room greeted her. "Pamela?"

The silence was deafening. Her gaze shot to the counter where her cell phone had been, her father's text message lighting up the screen. It was gone. In its place sat a note:

This is my chance to make things right. Be happy.

- Mom

Chapter Ten

Through his swollen right eye, Troy stared at the door of the motel room, begging Ruby not to walk through it. Part of him knew it was useless to hope. He could already see her storming in like an avenging angel, demanding to take his place. Her mother's place. She'd always been stubborn enough to believe she could fix the world. It was only one of the thousand or so reasons he loved her.

When they'd driven just past JFK airport and arrived at the motel room, he'd been at once relieved and unsurprised to find it empty. He'd suspected Jim of lying about Ruby and Pamela's being taken, but he'd refused to stake Ruby's life on a gut feeling. Now he sat on the floor with his back up against the wall, hands secured behind his back with his own cuffs. Jim had waited until Troy was without the use of his hands before clocking him over the head with the butt of his gun. Payment for warning Ruby over the phone. God, she'd sounded so damn scared. He'd never heard her sound like that, and the memory ricocheted though his brain, making him even dizzier.

Troy absently registered the feel of blood running down the side of his face as he glanced at the bedside clock. It had been forty minutes since Jim made the call. Within the space of twenty minutes, he could be dead, leaving Ruby to the mercy of her father.

The possibility of leaving her to fend for herself made him crazed.

When the knock sounded on the door, Troy braced himself against the wall, ready to move. He didn't know what would happen when Ruby walked in, but he needed to be prepared for anything.

Jim rose from the desk chair in which he'd been sitting, making notes on a horse racing form. Just before he pulled the door open, he turned and winked at Troy.

"Showtime."

The restraints around his wrists became unbearable. "You're a bastard."

Jim shrugged. "I've been called much worse."

He opened the door with a flourish to reveal Pamela. Troy strained to see past her, looking for Ruby, but he didn't see her. His mind raced, coming up with two possibilities. Either Ruby and Pamela were merely pretending to go along with Jim's wishes, or Pamela had ditched Ruby to sacrifice herself. *Jesus, please let her be safe somewhere, a million miles from this.*

"Pamela. It's been an age."

Ruby's mother pushed past Jim and strode into the motel room, holding up a leather knapsack. Seeing the arrogant walk so identical to Ruby's, Troy wondered how he'd missed their obvious relation for so long. It was right there in their demeanors, the way they stood as if ready to take on the world.

"Why don't we skip the small talk, Jimbo?"

A muscle ticked in his jaw. "Don't call me that."

"Fine." She tossed the knapsack onto the bed. "'Asshole' has a better ring to it anyway."

Jim smiled tightly. "Let's not forget who is holding the gun."

"You always were a one-upper." Her gaze connected with Troy, but he couldn't interpret anything from her expression. "Now, is this any way to treat your future son-in-law?"

"He's only a means to an end to me." Jim glanced back at the still partially open door. "Where's our daughter?"

"She's not coming," she said quickly. Too quickly. It told Troy she'd ditched Ruby in an attempt to do the right thing. A small part of him ached for her, knowing any sacrifice on her behalf would devastate Ruby, but his relief eclipsed the ache. "You were right. I've never done a damn thing for her. Figured this was the least I could do." She pointed at the bag on the bed. "Half of your money is in there. Let Troy go home to Ruby and I'll take you to the other half."

One of Jim's eyebrows rose. "You expect me to believe you've managed to hold on to all of it, without spending a dime?"

Pamela lifted one shoulder and let it fall. "I live thrifty. I even have a Costco membership."

Even in the midst of this fucked-up situation, Troy had to acknowledge the fact that Ruby had clearly gotten the smart-ass gene from her mother.

Jim tapped the gun against his thigh, considering Pamela through narrowed eyes. "Now, I'm a gambling man. And that's exactly what I'd be doing by walking out of this room on nothing but your word, giving you more time to run to the police and tell them what you saw." He tilted his head. "Too bad your word doesn't mean a rat's ass to me. Not to mention, I'd have to be a world-class idiot to let a do-gooder cop walk out of here after I've given him a mild concussion and threatened his life, as well as his girlfriend's."

"I wouldn't lie about this. I've had a good run, but I'm not going to make Ruby pay for my mistakes anymore. Our mistakes."

"How noble of you to make that decision for us."

She shifted on her feet, letting her nerves show for the first time. "Come on, Jim. Let Troy walk out of here and we'll go get your fifty grand."

Jim laughed. "You don't get it. I never really expected to get this money back, Pamela. This is about way more than money." He pointed the gun at her. "No, I'll take my fifty grand and cut my losses. And you're finally going to get what's coming to you."

• • •

Ruby threw a handful of money at the cab driver and sprinted from the vehicle the second it stopped moving. Not knowing which direction to go, she scanned the posted sign embedded in the motel's stucco wall and ran left through the deserted parking lot for room 225. Her heart thudded in her ears, stomach hollow with the worry that she'd come too late.

When she saw the door sitting slightly ajar, she slowed to a walk, terrified over what she would find on the other side. Her father's angry voice reached her then, telling her at least someone was still alive in there with him. She didn't give herself time to feel relief or worry over which person remained alive, her boyfriend or her mother. Allowing the thoughts to fester would only debilitate her, and she was racing the clock.

She took a deep breath and pushed open the door, taking in the entire scene in one wide-eyed glance. Pamela facing away, arms raised as her father pointed the gun at her head. Troy, bound and bloody against the wall. For one brief, horrifying section, she thought the blood pouring down his face came from a bullet wound, but then he saw her and tensed.

Deducing quickly that her mother was in the most danger, Ruby shot forward and inserted herself between Pamela and the gun, ignoring Troy's choked command to stop. Immediately, Jim lowered the gun, betraying himself. Despite everything he'd done to make her life hell, at least a tiny part of him cared about her. Enough that he didn't want to shoot her, at the very least. She needed to use that.

"Please, put the gun down."

Out of the corner of her eye, she saw Troy struggle to his feet. "Ruby, turn around and walk out of here. *Now*."

She gave a tiny shake of her head, not willing to lose sight of her father and the gun. "I can't. You know I can't."

Jim jerked his chin in Troy's direction. "Listen to him. I'll give you ten seconds, then all bets are off." His throat worked with rare emotion. "I'd rather not do this in front of you."

"Don't do it at all," she pleaded. "Please. Don't take them from me."

"This was in motion long before you were born. She knew better than to come back to New York. I spared her once. I can't do it again. Your boyfriend is just an unfortunate bystander." His eyes closed briefly. "Move out of the way, Ruby."

She swallowed hard. "No."

Jim heaved out a sigh. Then he pointed the gun at Troy.

Ruby's vision went black around the edges. "No. *No.*"

"There's two of them, Ruby, and only one of you. You can't do anything to stop it."

Ruby's panicked gaze connected with Troy. When she saw the resignation on his face, a sharp sound of grief escaped her lips. He nodded once, as if trying to reassure her. "It's okay, baby. It'll be okay." She jerked back around to find her father's finger tightening on the trigger. Ruby didn't think. She just moved, throwing herself across the room in front of Troy, shielding him from the inevitable bullet. At the last second, she saw something spark in his eyes. He'd anticipated her move, known exactly what she was going to do before she'd even processed it. Using his body, he spun her around and pinned her hard against the wall, his muscular frame jerking with the impact of the gunfire.

Her screamed denial was drowned out by the blood rushing in her ears. Troy inhaled shakily near her forehead, then dropped to his knees. She wrapped her arms around his midsection to keep him upright, but couldn't support his weight. When they both went down to the ground, Ruby could feel moisture rushing over her hands. Blood. "Oh, God. No. Troy, *no*."

Blue eyes dull with pain, he spoke. "You didn't do this, okay? Don't waste time...blaming yourself." He winced. "Fuck. I love you so much. You know that, right?"

"I love you, too." Tears streaming down her cheeks, she ripped off her shirt and pressed it against his wound. Troy was wrong. She *had* done this. From the moment they met, he'd been doomed to this fate simply by associating himself with her. *No, no, please don't let him die because of me.* She started praying under her breath, promising to whoever was listening that if Troy made it through this alive, she would leave him alone, exactly like she should have done in the first place. Once he was free of her, he would be safe. Far away from her past where it couldn't reach out and hurt him. "You're going to be okay. You *have* to. *Please,* Troy."

Over Troy's shoulder, she watched in slow motion as her mother took advantage of Jim's momentary distraction by hurtling herself into his body and knocking the gun free. It landed on the carpet inches from Ruby's leg, firing a wild shot into the wall just behind her, sending plaster flying everywhere. Pamela struggled with Jim to keep him from reaching the weapon, spurring Ruby into action. She picked the gun up and pointed it at Jim from her position on the floor, keeping the pressure on Troy's wound with her other hand. Her father froze, raising his hands toward the ceiling. Based on his cautious expression, Ruby knew her face betrayed the crazed anguish pummeling her insides.

"Call the police," she half sobbed, half shouted at Pamela. "Tell them to send an ambulance. Right now. Tell them Troy's a police officer." Anything to get them there faster. *Have to save him.*

She kept the gun trained on Jim as Pamela rushed to make the call, pulse jumping in alarm when Troy slumped over, appearing on the verge of unconsciousness. Her throat was on fire, a piercing buzz taking up residence in her skull. This couldn't be happening. When Pamela hung up, a tense silence hung in the room.

Jim took a step forward. "Ruby—"

"Why?" She cocked the gun with her thumb. "Why did you have to come back? Either of you."

Both of them stared at her in silence.

"Did you not do enough damage before? You had to come back and finish me off?" Her voice had risen to a shrill scream, but she didn't care. The love of her life was dying beside her on the floor. On some level, she knew she would die right along with him. "I was happy. We were *happy*. Why couldn't you just leave me alone?"

"I'm sorry," Pamela whispered. Jim looked away. For a split second, Ruby even saw regret coast over his features, but she hardened herself against it.

Sirens pierced the air. Ruby judged them to be about half a mile away. *Come on. Hurry.*

"Ruby, I'm not going to jail." Her father turned slowly and picked up the leather knapsack. "I'm walking out that door. You can either shoot me or let me go."

Her hand shook under the weight of the gun, so she added her other hand for support. "Give me one reason why I shouldn't pull the trigger."

Jim started to talk, but his gaze was drawn by Troy's hand on her arm. "Don't do it," he wheezed. "You're better than him, Ruby."

A sob ripped from her throat when she saw how gray his complexion had turned. "If I'm better, it's only because of you."

Troy shook his head, then slowly his eyelids drooped as he lost consciousness. Ruby shouted an intelligible curse at the ceiling, saved from complete insanity by the sirens drawing closer. She turned back to her father in time to see his shock, seemingly over witnessing her so distraught. As if he hadn't realized how deeply her feelings ran for Troy.

You have no idea. You don't know how *to feel.*

The rational part of her knew Troy was right, but she felt anything but rational at that moment. As her father backed toward the door, she wanted to pull the trigger. Desperately. Just to end it. Make sure he couldn't cause any more pain. But something held her back. "If he dies," she grated, "I will find you."

Something unnamed but poignant passed between them.

Jim nodded once, hefting the knapsack onto his shoulder. Then he was gone.

Chapter Eleven

Ruby's voice echoed in Troy's head, fervent prayers being delivered in frantic, pleading whispers. His body felt like it was floating, his senses dull. Nothing seemed to be working apart from his memory, which wouldn't leave him alone. Or was Ruby saying these words in the present and he simply couldn't open his eyes to see her? With an iron will, he lifted his hand, reaching for her, but it only landed on a cold sheet. Then the beeping intruded. Muffled voices. Irritation filled his chest. He wanted to shout at everyone to be quiet so he could hear what Ruby was trying to tell him.

Please, please, don't let him die. I'll leave him alone. I swear I'll stay away from him. Just please, let him live. I'll do anything.

His eyes flew open, although they felt weighted down and rubbed raw. He searched for Ruby in the dim room, but he couldn't see her anywhere. *Leave me alone?*

Panic seized him, carrying another memory in its wake. His mother standing at the foot of his bed, trying to console an emotional Ruby before she apologized with sickening finality and ran from the room. The sticky fog lifted from its position around his brain, just as the beeping accelerated into a blur.

She'd left him.

Troy couldn't think past that single thought. It didn't matter that she'd promised to stay away from him in the heat of the moment. Or that this was her misguided attempt to do the right thing. Troy couldn't move past the thought of not having her.

Faces entered his line of vision. Some unfamiliar, some he recognized, but he didn't want to listen or acknowledge their rushed commands for him to lie still. He needed to get to her. If she thought she could walk away, he would merely inform her of the opposite until she understood. As he struggled past the sea of arms and startled voices to get to his feet, sharp tugs in his arms and back hindered his progress. He gritted his teeth and yanked at the obstacles. The roaring pain that followed was secondary to the one in his heart.

"Officer Bennett, you're in the hospital. You've been shot." Irrelevant words he didn't have the wherewithal to attach to a face. "You must lie down or you will open your stitches."

"*Where…is she?*"

"Who?"

"Ruby." His mother's voice broke in impatiently. "He's asking for his girlfriend."

His girlfriend. His world. His breath. "*Ruby.*"

As though he'd conjured her with a single word, he heard a door slam and then everything came into focus. He saw her coming toward him, a single hand outstretched. Troy reached out and grabbed it like a lifeline, pulling her toward the bed. Toward him. Her clothes were covered in blood and his head swam with terrible fear before he remembered it was his own. Then she was in his arms and he could think of nothing else. Not the pain in his back or the buzzing in his head. Just her.

"Officer Bennett," the doctor interrupted as three nurses rushed into the room. "You've opened your stitches. I'm going to administer a painkiller and sedative now so we can repair the damage. Here it comes."

"Troy." Ruby's voice shook. "Let them take care of you. Please."

His mouth felt dry as everything around him slowed. He no longer had the strength to keep his arms around Ruby, and he hated letting her go. "I need you here when I wake up."

"I'm not going anywhere."

His world went black once more.

• • •

With a start, he woke again in the darkness, but felt immediate comfort when he registered the unmistakable weight of Ruby's hand curled inside his own. *She didn't leave. She's here. Thank God.* She'd fallen asleep facing him, her hair fanned out on his hospital bed. A soft green glow had been cast by the machines, illuminating her just enough for Troy to see how exhausted she looked. He squeezed her hand and attempted a smile as her eyes slowly came open and focused on him.

"Hi." She pushed her dark tangle of hair away from her exhausted face. "H-how do you feel?"

He tried to read her expression and failed. Her earlier promises assaulted him once more, only now they were twice as sharp and clear. *I'll leave him alone.* "I'm not going to lie, I've felt better." When guilt flashed across her features, he tilted her chin up with his hand. "Please talk to me."

She cast a watery glance toward the ceiling. "I can't stop feeling the bullet hit you. Seeing your eyes...watching you fall..."

He cradled her cheek in his hand. "We came through it alive and together. Let's focus on that." A broken sound escaped her throat, and it sent a surge of fear straight to his gut. The possibility of a loss greater than his life stole his breath. "Ruby, you don't get to leave me."

For a painfully long moment, she simply stared at him. "Good. Because I couldn't do it." A tear tracked down her cheek. "I tried to do the right thing, but I'm too selfish."

"Dammit," Troy started, stark relief dulling his pulse as it beat in his ears. "I don't like hearing that you tried to leave me."

"I *should* leave." Her breath shuddered out. "More than that, you should want me to."

"No. *Never.*"

She reached out to trace her thumb over his bottom lip. "I didn't make it one block, Troy. Not one block."

Hearing the same words he'd spoken to her all those months ago, his heart slammed into his ribs, feeling as though it might burst. "Good," he managed shakily. "That's good."

"I've never been so scared in my life," she whispered. "And that's saying something."

Their gazes held for a long moment before he tugged her to her feet. "Crawl in here. I've spent way too many nights without you lately."

"Troy, your parents are in the hallway," she scoffed, shaking her head. "And you haven't even met the nurse yet. I thought *I* didn't take anyone's shit."

With a frown, he lifted the sheet on his good side. "In."

Ruby sighed through her smile, then climbed onto the hospital bed so gingerly he had to laugh. When she laid her head on his shoulder, a sense of rightness flooded him. Scenes from the motel room rose unbidden in his mind. "What happened to Jim? After I…"

Her body tensed, so he rubbed circles into her back. "I… let him go. I just couldn't do it."

Troy felt thankful. "You did the right thing, baby."

"Did I?" She traced a pattern on his chest. "When I look at you lying here attached to a bunch of machines, I'm not so sure."

"You did," Troy countered firmly. "Never question that."

She propped herself up on her elbow and kissed him softly. "Troy, you took a bullet for me. I don't know whether to be mad as hell or fall even deeper in love with you."

"I'll take option two."

"Good." Her voice resonated with sincerity. "Because I'm yours until the end, Troy Bennett."

Love burning in his chest, he brushed his lips over hers. "Then I hope the end never comes."

Epilogue

Ruby closed the door behind her mother and leaned against it for a moment. With a small smile, she turned and began to clear dishes from the table. Dinner had gone well. In the three weeks since Troy had been shot, they had made significant progress. They'd talked about the past in bits and pieces, although one of them usually changed the subject before the conversation turned too heavy. Their relationship would never be even remotely conventional. Thank God.

For the last three weeks, taking care of Troy had been Ruby's number one priority, not to mention, her pleasure. She'd been working at home as much as she could, only running to the workshop to pick up supplies, or relying on Pamela to drop off new work orders. Before her father had returned, she'd thought her relationship with Troy was strong, their bond unbreakable. Now, however, their strength as a couple had increased tenfold. They had even begun communicating in new, subtler ways, through touches and simple intuition. The terror of nearly losing him, that emptiness she'd felt on the ambulance ride to the hospital when he'd been bloody and unconscious, had forced her to acknowledge feelings she'd never realized existed. Troy was a part of her. They held each other's hearts in their hands. Exposed, and yet completely safe.

She would never again, for a single second, take that kind of love for granted.

By the time she'd told Troy about Bowen being her half brother, his jealousy had become merely an afterthought. Something irrelevant and in their past. He'd even tried to help her locate Bowen, to thank him or even just to talk, but her wayward sibling wasn't ready to be found just yet. They hadn't seen him since that night in the alley behind Mancuso's.

She hadn't told Troy about the look she'd shared with Bowen. It wasn't one she could interpret or put into words, nor did she understand it, anyway. But it came with the certainty that, unless she fought and pushed, her relationship with her half brother had ended in that alley.

So someday very soon, she *would* fight. Like she'd been taught. Like *hell*.

Ruby put the final dish on the drying rack just as Troy's arms slipped around her waist. Complete. She felt so complete. Her fingers trembled when she thought of how close she'd come to never being held by him again. Never encountering his scent, his voice, his solid form. Every time she closed her eyes for the last three weeks, the what-ifs came. Would they ever stop?

"You okay, baby? You're cold."

"I'm fine, I just—"

A loud thump against the front door of their apartment sent a jolt zigzagging like lightning through her middle. She didn't know why such an innocuous sound alarmed her to such a degree, but it did. It sharpened her instincts like two blades striking against each other. Troy's body stiffening behind her told Ruby he shared her concern.

Without making a sound, Troy reached around her hip to open a kitchen drawer, taking out his department-issued Glock and turning off the safety. He laid a soft kiss on her forehead. "Everything is going to be fine."

With a stilted nod, she disengaged from Troy and followed him slowly toward the front door, ignoring the nightmarish image of it swinging open, some unnamed danger rushing in. Watching Troy get hurt again, when he finally stood so solid and reassuring before her. With a finger pressed to his lips, reminding her to stay silent, Troy looked through the peephole into their building's hallway, his blue eyes showing no signs of seeing anything lurking on the other side. After positioning himself in front of her, he turned the dead bolt and opened the door.

Sitting on the floor near her feet sat the leather knapsack her father had fled the motel room with three weeks prior.

She dragged the heavy bag inside, and Troy bolted the door closed behind them. Opening it in the manner that one would rip off a Band-Aid, she gaped at the contents. Money. So much money. She took quick stock of the neat stacks. Fifty thousand dollars. Her father had come back, at his own risk... to give it to her? A message. But what kind? Was this his way of apologizing? The little girl inside her wanted to weep, grateful that he'd thought of her. Wondering if the gesture meant he loved her, even a little.

The woman inside her wanted to burn it.

"What do you want to do?"

Keeping the money never even crossed her mind. "Do you think we could find someone who needs it? Maybe through the police..."

"Of course we can. Tomorrow." He took her hand, pride shining in his eyes. She let him pull her into his side and lead her away from the door. Always protecting. Placing himself between her and the danger. Halfway to the kitchen, Troy pulled her back against his chest. "What were you thinking about before? In the kitchen."

No secrets. "I almost lost you," she whispered. "The fear. It'll never go away."

He made a gruff sound. "I'm here." His warm breath sent a shiver vibrating through her belly. "Let me show you how much I'm here."

Automatically, her head tilted to the side so his lips could run up the side of her neck. When one warm hand pressed against her abdomen, bringing her bottom back onto his lap, Ruby groaned.

"You know we can't, Troy. One more week until the doctor clears you."

He ignored her, snapping open the button of her jeans. "I'm very aware of how much longer you'll be playing my nurse, baby. I'm enjoying every single second of it." His fingers slipped beneath the waistband of her panties, one finger delving deep inside her. "But I've also had way too much time to fantasize about fucking my bossy nurse whose uniform consists of goddamn panties and a T-shirt. I can't wait another week to play them out. I can't."

Her breath hitched when he used the dampness he'd gathered to massage her clit. Three weeks was the longest they'd gone without each other since they'd met. God, she needed him, too. So damn bad. As soon as his color had returned to normal and he'd been able to walk without being hunched over, she'd started feeling breathless every time they were in the same room. It had been about a week of lingering touches and going to bed sexually frustrated. Troy hadn't made it any easier, insisting he would deal with any amount of pain to be inside her, filling her ear with sensual promises as they lay in bed. *It hurts, Ruby. Climb on and fix me.*

She'd been the sole voice of reason in the house. But her patience had started to wear dangerously thin.

"Are you s-sure?" she asked now.

With a growl of triumph, he unzipped her jeans and yanked them down her hips. A few seconds later, she heard his own jeans hit the floor, the clank of his falling belt sending shivers racing across her skin. "Am I sure, Ruby?" Then he was walking her forward and turning them as they reached the kitchen table. He fell into one of the chairs and brought her down on his lap. In one rough move, he'd sunk deep inside her. Their simultaneous moans ricocheted through the kitchen. "Do I feel sure enough to you?"

"Oh *God*, yes."

Ruby kicked off her jeans the rest of the way so she could drape her legs over his thighs, pushing him even deeper, to the hilt. Then she braced her hands on his knees and began to work her body up and down his stiff erection.

Already, she could feel her stomach muscles tightening. He felt huge inside her, touching her everywhere, stimulating her every sense. "Does that...feel okay?"

He ran desperate hands up the insides of her thighs. "You never feel anything less than perfect, but hell, three weeks without me has done you good, hustler. It feels like I've got a fucking virgin riding me."

With a scream of relief, she went hurtling into a shaking climax. Her hips bucked to get her through it, wringing every last ounce of sensation from her aching body. When it passed, her bones felt liquefied, but she could still feel Troy hard inside her. Hands on her shoulders, he drew her swiftly back against his heaving chest.

"Don't you dare stop." Her T-shirt was ripped over her head and tossed to the floor. When his hands molded to her breasts, another wave of heat rushed through her. "Don't slow down. Don't rest for a goddamn second. Not until you've satisfied your patient."

"Yes, Troy." She planted her feet on the floor and

increased the pace of her hips, letting him slip out until only his thick tip remained inside her, then sinking back down with a wicked twist of her body. Over and over until she heard his groans of pleasure grow uneven behind her. The fingertips of one hand dug roughly into the flesh of her thigh, telling Ruby how close he was to release. She cried out his name when he used the other hand to pet the sensitive spot between her legs, once again sending her racing toward a mind-bending climax.

"Fuck, I'm almost gone." He wrapped her hair in his fist and turned her head to the side. "You know what I want to hear while I'm coming. Say it."

She licked her parted lips. "I love you. So much. I...*ah*."

His orgasm sent her flying into another one, somehow more intense because she could see his eyes glaze over as it overtook her. She watched him throw his head back and shout her name at the ceiling with such intensity, her chest felt crowded with emotion.

Troy's voice bathed her ear in heat. "I love you, too. Until the end."

She turned and kissed his lips. "Until the end."

Acknowledgments

To my husband, Patrick, and daughter, Mackenzie, I love you both. I would never have started writing again without your love, support and encouragement.

To Heather Howland, who upon seeing my post in Bailey's Babes about the possible continuation of HIS RISK TO TAKE, texted me with, "Okay, write me a sequel. Now." Best text ever.

To my father, who taught me how to play pool as a young girl. Those pool tournaments between you and Pop are some of my best memories. I'll carry them with me forever.

To Bailey's Babes, sometimes I think your encouragement is what keeps these characters alive. Thank you, thank you, thank you.

To beautiful, broken boys like Bowen for showing up in books and stealing my heart, until I have no choice but to base an entire series around them, thank you. This is why I write.

About the Author

New York Times and *USA TODAY* bestselling author Tessa Bailey lives in Brooklyn, New York, with her husband and young daughter. When she isn't writing or reading romance, she enjoys a good argument and thirty-minute recipes.

www.tessabailey.com

Join Bailey's Babes!

Discover more Entangled Select Suspense titles...

BURNOUT

an *NYPD Blue & Gold* novel by Tee O'Fallon

Sexy-as-sin Police Chief Mike Flannery knows the new arrival to Hopewell Springs is trouble; he's been a cop too long not to recognize the signs of a woman running from her past. But he can't resist her quick wit, smoking-hot body, and the easy way she embraces their close-knit community. NYPD Detective Cassie Yates is on the run. Armed with fake ID, her K-9, and a police-issued SUV, she flees to this quiet upstate town to avoid a hit. When the hired assassin hunts her down, Mike's past comes roaring back and secrets are revealed in an explosion destined to tear them apart—if not destroy them.

ON HER SIX

an *Under Covers* novel by Christina Elle

New neighbors are bad news in Samantha Harper's experience. Especially ones as suspicious and brooding as the guy who just moved in next door. So when the dangerous but sexy stranger seems to be involved in something illegal—the aspiring cop in her takes action. All DEA agent Ash Cooper wants to do is lay low and survive this crap surveillance assignment. But after a run-in with his attractive neighbor, he realizes that's going to be much harder than he planned. Keeping the woman out of trouble is hard enough, but keeping his hands off her is near impossible.

STRANGER IN MY HOUSE
a *Murder in Texas* novel by Mari Manning

When Kirby Swallow assumes her half sister's identity to help figure out who's threatening her, she finds herself in way over her head. On the remote Texas ranch her sister calls home, she confronts a growing list of suspects and a rising body count. The only problem is the sexy ranch manager, Seth Maguire, is starting to catch on to the charade. The attraction between them is undeniable. But someone on the ranch is out for blood...and Kirby's next.

IMPOSSIBLE RANSOM
a novel by Kathleen Mix

Working as part of a yacht crew sounded like the perfect escape for senator's daughter Val Ferrell. But when the ship is hijacked, Val's fantasy turns into a nightmare. Her only hope is the ship's captain, her ex-lover. Covert operative Nick O'Shea is working with the tiny blonde who makes him crazy. But when her life is endangered, Nick must choose between fighting to retake the boat or risking their lives by escaping to an isolated Caribbean island. With the ransom deadline rapidly approaching, he's running out of time...

Printed in the USA
CPSIA information can be obtained
at www.ICGtesting.com
LVHW090446151123
763986LV00064B/1585